SMALL DREAMS HAVE NO MAGIC

The Key to Success

SMALL DREAMS HAVE NO

MAGIC

The Key to Success

ROGER F. JOHNSRUD

SUCCESS MOTIVATION ADVENTURE MYSTERY STORY

For Ages 8 to 80

ARPress
45 Dan Road Suite 36
Canton MA 02021

Hotline: 1(888) 821-0229
Fax: 1(508) 545-7580

Ordering Information:
Quantity Sales. Special discounts are available on quantity purchases by corporations, associations, and others. For details, contact the publisher at the address above.

Printed in the United States of America.

ISBN-13   Paperback   979-8-89356-917-9
                      eBook   979-8-89356-919-3
                      Hardback   979-8-89356-918-6

Library of Congress Control Number: 2024905478

DEDICATION

This book is dedicated to my daughter Theresa. She helped me to realize that children must be taught the secrets of success before they grow old.

The book is a memorial to my two daughters Judy and Jody, taken from me before I was taught the secrets of success and the prayer that they may someday know the true spirit of their father.

The book is also dedicated to my two sons Edward and Kenneth. Though they have endured much suffering, I hope they know the key to success is within their grasp.

I dedicate this book to my late wife Jeanith. Though she suffered painfully medically for many years, she has taught me never to give up.

I would also like to dedicate this book to my youngest daughter Kimberly that has grown into a wonderful young woman with all the ambition and understanding to succeed.

I would also like to dedicate this revision to Melody for the many years of unbelievable support through the worst and best times.

I would like to dedicate this book to my late younger brother Ralph, who is preparing the way for my next journey to eternity.

And last, I want to dedicate this book to all the children eight to eighty so that they may have the Key to Success without waiting any longer.

Grand embellishments Of castle walls …

What makes you think you could be someone different than who you are?

FORWARD

What would you do if you found a little black book that revealed the true secrets of success? How would you react to the innocuous yet mysterious phrases, brimming with hidden meanings, which awaited you the first day? Naturally your aroused curiosity would drive you to read another phrase the next day, and the cycle would go on.

In *Small Dreams have no Magic (The Key to Success),* author Roger F. Johnsrud gives us Jonathan, a young stable worker, who finds, *"The Key to Success",* a book which seems to hold the magical power to bring him the success he so greatly desires. Jonathan lives in a time long ago when kingdom-based societies flourish and selfless goodwill abounds in daily life.

By chance he meets Heather, a young woman who holds the promises to a new life in the form of a homemade secret formula. Jonathan risks his future by leaving his job to run a business with Heather and his friends.

Along the way, Jonathan acquires the respect of noblemen and the generous assistance of local businessmen, gathering new friends and assistance while looking to build the business and doing his best to understand the magic within the book.

Small Dreams Have No Magic is invigorating and rewarding, while at the same time educational and spiritually uplifting. The author creates his characters and story line in such a way as to teach us very important moral directives about avoiding the negative temptations of life, helping those that try to help themselves, and never letting determination slip away in the fear that our dreams won't come true.

For all ages 8 to 80

"This book will help you "Own Your Own Life" and <u>Live Your Dreams</u> sooner than you might think. The magic in this book will amaze you. You will be successful in whatever you choose. Read it today and share it with a friend."

Don and Nancy Failla
---"International Networking Trainers"

TABLE OF CONTENTS

Chapter 1
The Key

Jonathan woke up confused. It was late evening, and he was propped up in a tree. There was a sound of an argument in the meadow below.

Now he remembered, he had journeyed out in the late afternoon to hunt the large deer he had seen the day before in the forest. At least he did not need to worry about being an outlaw like the stories of Robin Hood. This was not the king's forest, and the king was a good king.

He had decided to rest in the tree over the small clearing so that a wild boar would not attack him. He must have fallen asleep while waiting for the deer.

But what was the commotion below him? His eyes strained for a better view in the dim light. Three hags shouted at the small old man. "Give us the key!"

The man was dressed in a long cloak with an attached hood that covered his entire face except for the glow of his eyes in the firelight. He was sitting down with his legs crossed and he was bound with heavy twine. The old hags poked the old man with a stick and hot coals from the fire. Their torture was constant and with great pleasure. They continuously berated the man to give them the key.

Jonathan was about to offer a gallant rescue and was preparing to jump from the tree. Suddenly there was a loud clap of thunder and a big puff of smoke. Instantly the man disappeared into a pile of ashes. The incident startled Jonathan. He was glad he had not interfered once he realized the ominous powers that lurked below.

What was the key? Where did the man go? Who were these three hideous creatures? His fear was strong but the desire to know more kept him attentive to every detail.

The clamor of the hags became louder than ever. They threw so much wood on the fire that the flames almost reached Jonathan in his high perch. The campfire was so bright that Jonathan could see the sweat on his arm. *What if they saw him? To be banished to smoke was the best thought he had.*

He strained hard to remain perfectly still. His legs were stiff, but he dared not risk moving for fear that a small piece of falling bark would draw the witch's attention. *What were they doing? Why were they sifting through the ashes of the old man, digging around the campsite, and muttering all the while,* "Where is the key?"

It seemed like days before the old hags lost interest, but Jonathan knew it was only the eternity of the night. Even after they had gone and the sun was up for several hours, Jonathan found it difficult to stray from his nest.

Eventually Jonathan's curiosity drew him down for he could not resist the search for the key. *What power could the key hold that would compare to the magic of turning a man to dust? Imagine what he could do with such power? Ah, but only witches and wizards have such magic.*

Slowly Jonathan started for home, yet his eyes constantly searched the bright green forest. When he turned toward the town, a glint of gold under a bush caught his eye.

A moment of excitement surged though him as he raced to the shrub and reached for a small leather covered book. His eyes widened as he read the golden title aloud, "The Key to Success". The feeling ebbed quickly, and depression overcame him when he realized that it was a book with no more than a handful of pages. *Surely it could not hold any significant value, especially for the powerful witches.*

There must be some other key.

The book was a small, black leather, handsomely bound manuscript with only a couple of dozen pages. Each page held a simple sentence or two in old Gothic script. Jonathan opened the book and read the first page.

"MANY HAVE READ THIS AND ALL CAN SUCCEED, A DEEPER UNDERSTANDING IS ALL THAT YOU NEED."

Jonathan was miffed at the whimsical poetry, yet he proceeded by turning the page and read the first chapter, though he could hardly call one sentence a chapter.

"DREAMS ARE FOR REAL PEOPLE PRACTICING MAGIC AT NIGHT, WHY SHOULD YOU BE DIFFERENT AND LIVE ONLY IN LIGHT?"

Jonathan was amused and confused by what he had read. *He dreamed at night, and it was silly to believe that he was alive only in the light.*

As Jonathan shoved the book into his pack, *he wondered if he would be able to sell the book to someone. Possibly he could trick the witches into believing the book was really the key they were looking for and make a handsome profit before they realized their mistake.* At the same time as Jonathan walked down the path to town, he could not help thinking about the book. *What if the book did hold the key to success?*

He thought about the many people he knew that were successful. *The baker was successful. He had his own shop and a nice house. Why should the baker have more than Jonathan? Why shouldn't he, though presently only a lowly stable boy, have as much as the baker? The blacksmith*

and the miller were also successful. What about the king's knights, the Baron, or the king himself? Why, if he had even part of their success, he would be incredibly happy.

Jonathan, while walking, *imagined himself as a knight riding a gallant white horse and holding a bright shiny shield.* He was startled awake when he bumped into a fat old man.

"What are you doing boy?" asked the fryer, "Trying to run me down? Where is your mind? Are you dreaming during the day?"

Jonathan excused himself, picked up the green triangular cap that had fallen from his head, and proceeded through the gates of the stable.

He was more than two hours late for work and knew he needed an excuse. *He decided the truth was best, so he started his story before the stable master had a chance to ask him where he had been.*

"Now your imagination is running wild before you get to work!" quipped the stable master. "If you want success, keep the stable clean. What right do you have to be someone different than who you are?"

Well, it was true. The best he was expected to do was to become stable master someday. But what if ...?

It was late and already dark when Jonathan finished his work. He stood quietly at the door as he looked at the night sky. *There seemed to be an unusual number of stars tonight and he wondered if there were more stars than those he could see? The moon was only half full, but for some strange reason he noticed the dark circular outline of the rest of the moon. He had never noticed it before, and he thought what else is around me that I have never seen.*

Suddenly, a moment of inspiration overcame him. *The book was right! You need to dream a little and pay attention to everything around you. You do not need to be what you appear to be.*

His hands were shaking while he fumbled through his pack for the book. What would have happened if he had given the book to the witches? The words took on a new meaning as he realized the power of success may very well be in only a few words.

Chapter 2
Visions

Quickly Jonathan turned the pages to the second chapter. It was hard to read the book in the dark, but the moon provided just enough light to see the next few lines.

"VISIONS OF THE PAST TAKE THE FUTURE TO TASK. VISIONS OF TOMORROW STOP THE PAIN AND BRING NO SORROW."

Jonathan was tired. It had, after all, been a day and a half since he had slept. He climbed into the loft, crawled into his bed, and closed his eyes. He must sleep now since the stable will be busy tomorrow. In fact, the stable will be busy for the next month due to the fair that will be starting within two weeks. *"This month would be like last year, lots of work and no rest,"* he thought.

He soon fell asleep, and the only sounds heard in the stable were crickets and the rustle of hay as the horses moved to get more comfortable.

The chickens cackling at the sound of a trumpet woke Jonathan two hours earlier than usual. Last year the cart for the hay broke a wheel the first day of the busy season. *Jonathan imagined that if the wheel did not break this year, then something else bad would happen.*

He tossed around in his makeshift bed refusing to get up only to think of another problem. The minutes seemed to take hours. *He wondered if the water bucket would leak as badly as last month.* He kept it immersed in water so that it would swell up and slow the leaking. By the time he carried the bucket from the stream to the water trough, the bucket was only half full. If it leaked any more, it would take him three trips to make one bucket.

Jonathan rolled over, restlessly trying to sleep, but he could only think of the wasted time. It takes fifteen minutes to go to the stream and fetch a bucket of water. It takes two trips to get one bucket to the trough because the bucket leaks. That means a half hour per bucket, and it takes at least ten buckets to fill the trough. *"My gosh," thought Jonathan. "I spend five to seven hours a day just watering the darn horses!"*

In mindless thought, he watched a small bug crawl across the ceiling. Instantly Jonathan came to his senses. *"What if I repaired the bucket? It would only take a couple hours and I could save two or three hours a day fetching water. What a difference two to three hours a day would make in my life. I could finish my work early and spend a few hours a day learning a new trade or even how to do business."*

Jonathan jumped out of bed and shouted, *"The book is right again! I cannot bother myself with past problems that only slow me down today. I need to plan ahead and get started now."*

Jonathan smiled at his own wisdom and jumped to his feet saying, *"I need to fix the bucket this morning and start saving my time today. Sometimes the key to success comes easy."*

Jonathan dressed quickly and raced to the water trough to fetch the bucket. Within an hour the bucket was repaired. Jonathan felt good knowing the task was done long before he normally woke up. He was looking forward to what he could do today with the extra couple of hours he had already saved. *"This is the biggest pay raise I have ever received. Just think, the same pay for a lot less work,"* sang Jonathan.

Chapter 3
Who We Are

Jonathan went back to the hayloft and reached for his pack lying close to his blanket. He pulled the book out of the pack and turned to the next chapter.

"THE ONLY DIFFERENCE FOR ME IS YOU, AND THE SAME FOR YOU IS ME. DO YOU WANT ME DIFFERENT BECAUSE OF YOU, OR YOU BECAUSE OF ME?"

This did not strike Jonathan as an easy riddle to solve. He carefully placed the book back in his pack. This time he would be a little more careful with the treasure now in his possession. He raced to the stable yard to start his day while pondering the words he had just read.

Jonathan was whistling on his way to the stream for a new bucket of water when he came upon Jeffrey from the flour mill.

"Why are you so happy?" queried Jeffrey.

"I just received a pay raise and some time off," replied Jonathan.

"Great," said Jeffrey. "How about taking a few minutes for breakfast? Maybe we can stop by and ask Michael at the beverage stand to come along."

Jonathan and Jeffrey proceeded to the beverage stand and talked small talk all the way. Jonathan wanted to say something to Jeffrey about the book, but he was not sure if Jeffrey would believe him. Besides Jonathan was not sure the book was anything special anyway.

They finally reached the beverage stand and Jonathan asked, "Michael where do you want to eat?" They could not make up their minds if they wanted pies or just to eat at the beverage stand.

"Let's eat pies," said Michael. "I don't want to eat at my own beverage stand." After eating the pies, the young men planned their next few days of activity.

"Should we practice archery or watch the Knights practice for the fair?" asked Michael.

"What do you think?" asked Jeffrey.

"I would like to watch the Knights," replied Jonathan.

"Okay with us," answered Jeffrey and Michael.

"I need to return to work," said Jonathan. "There is a lot to do before the fair starts and the day has just begun." Jonathan turned toward the stable lost in thought. "I think I know what the book was saying," muttered Jonathan.

"What book?" asked Jeffrey.

Jonathan smiled slyly and said. "Walk by the pond while I fetch some water and I will explain."

The three boys headed for the pond and Jonathan explained, "We ate breakfast because of you Jeffrey, we eat pies because Michael wanted to eat pies, then we decided to watch the Knights because I wanted to watch them, and you are going to the pond because I suggested we go. Don't you see, my life is different because of what you want, and you do things different because of me!"

"Very interesting, but what about this book?" said Jeffrey.

"It is the Key to Success, and I will soon be rich," quipped Jonathan.

Both Jeffrey and Michael started to laugh. "You will not be rich; you are only a stable boy and not even the stable master is rich!" shouted Jeffrey.

The young men walked away leaving Jonathan in thought. Jonathan did not notice the stable master when he entered the shed. "Hey boy, take this broom and put a little STRAWdust in your eyes instead of STARdust!" laughed the stable master. "You were born to be a stable boy not a Knight."

Jonathan smiled with joy. "Should I be rich, or should I be poor? What do you think?" asked Jonathan.

"Of course, you will always be poor," replied the stable master.

"That is the real secret," said Jonathan. "I do not have to be what you think or want me to be, I can and will be what I think, and I will be successful."

Jonathan merrily started to sweep the room. He had an inner sense of security and a newfound feeling of power. He thought, *"Maybe I should add to the chapter,* MOST PEOPLE LET WHAT THEY SEE CONTROL THEIR MIND, BUT SUCCESSFUL PEOPLE LET THEIR MIND CREATE WHAT OTHER PEOPLE SEE."

Chapter 4
Imagination

Jonathan took a piece of cheese and some bread and sat down for lunch in the loft. While eating he opened the book to another chapter and read,

"THE ONLY DIFFERENCE BETWEEN A GREAT IMAGINATION, A WILD IMAGINATION, AND NO IMAGINATION IS HOMOGENIZATION."

Jonathan decided that he was going to discover the answer to this riddle as soon as possible, and what better place to start his search than with the storyteller. Certainly, he must have a good imagination.

On the way to the pond for more water Jonathan stopped by the storyteller. "Oh, great storyteller, tell me what is the key to success regarding imagination?" asked Jonathan.

"I do not know," replied the storyteller. "I can tell you what it is not. The beggar has no imagination. He sits around all day, drinks wine, and complains about never having a job or opportunity. If he were given a beverage stand, a flour mill or stable, he would not have the imagination to keep it running."

Jonathan wanted to be fair to the beggar so on the way back from the pond he stopped by the intersection where the beggar always hung out. "Old man," asked Jonathan. "Tell me what you know about success regarding imagination."

"I do not know," replied the beggar. "I can tell you what it is not, the storyteller, he has a wild imagination. I remember many years ago the storyteller started to build a beverage stand, then he started a stable, then he started a flour mill. He never knew which one to work on. Every day he would change his mind and soon he failed."

Jonathan thanked the old man and continued back to the stable. He was pleased to find the Baron was just picking up his stallion. Jonathan had confidence now, so he asked the Baron, "Sir, tell me what you know about success regarding imagination."

The Baron replied, "All I can do is tell you what I did. I had a dream to build a stable, a beverage stand, and a flour mill. I knew I could not undertake all of that at one time, so I decided to start with the beverage stand. Soon I was making a small profit. I used the money to hire someone to manage the beverage stand and the rest was used as a down payment on an old stable. As a matter of fact, it was this stable. As time passed the stable became successful after a lot of work, I hired a stable master. My new profits were used to buy a broken flour mill. I finally repaired the mill and turned it into a success. Since that time my profits have been used to buy land."

Jonathan thanked the Baron and poured the water into the trough. Jonathan knew he had found another secret. *All three men had the same idea but only one had a plan and then focused on the project at hand.*

Chapter 5
Dreams

The day had been long, and Jonathan was tired. He was ready for bed and looked forward to a good night's sleep. Before going to bed, he opened his pack one more time to read another chapter from the "Key to Success". He was beginning to believe that only a few basic rules could make a person really successful.

"DREAMS ARE FOR CHILDREN, THEY ALWAYS COME TRUE. MAKE BELIEVE THIS TIME AND WATCH IT CHANGE YOU."

"Well," thought Jonathan. "I have dreams and so do a lot of older people. My dreams are just dreams, they do not come true."

That night as Jonathan slept, he dreamt about being a stable master. This was the same dream that he had as a small boy, but tonight it was much more vivid. Also, he had a dream about working around the castle. When he was small, he lived far in the country and had only heard about the castle. Now he was older and worked daily in the shadow of the castle. He dreamed of playing by a pond and working for a rich man. Now he worked for the Baron and visited the pond daily.

Jonathan awoke partially because he was very thirsty and partly because of the dreams. *Why was he having such dreams?*

He fell back to sleep quickly. **After a short time, he awoke suddenly again because of a vivid dream about being a famous land Baron. He was helping the poor peasants achieve success.**

Instantly Jonathan said to himself, *"WHAT WE BELIEVE CREATES OUR REALITY. Our mind cannot tell the difference between a dream and reality since the mind always creates reality. I now live and work where I used to dream. The castle was the ambition of the King and the dream of the architect. The moat was a vision of a military strategist. The roads and cities were not a product of nature but produced by the dreams of people. Truly what I dream can come true if I believe."*

Jonathan decided he would be much more careful in the future about what he thought since he now knew that what he thought was what he may become.

Chapter 6
Sands of Time

The morning sun was bright in Jonathan's eyes and as he awoke, he found himself reaching unconsciously for the pack. It was almost a habit to read the next chapter and try to solve the next riddle. Even though Jonathan was starting to understand the riddles, what he read in the next chapter made him think a little more than usual.

"THE SANDS OF TIME CAN BE BLOWN AWAY BUT ONLY ON A WINDY DAY."

Jonathan's mind wandered into an early morning daydream. He thought about his last trip to the ocean. The waves washed continuously over the sand and the sand must have been washed away. The wind was not necessary. He thought about a painting of the desert. The wind was definitely blowing the sand away, but it would surely take a long time.

Jonathan came back to reality as Smokey, a black cat, raced through the hay. Smokey stopped as suddenly as he appeared and lay quietly in the corner. He was after a mouse for sure and he usually did a good job. Often though Jonathan would see him sitting for a long time before a mouse would reappear. This cat was a good mouser and much better than the rest of the cats in the stable.

Jonathan slipped on his clothes, grabbed the bucket, and headed for the pond. Getting water was much easier now that the bucket was fixed, and the trips seemed shorter just knowing he would not lose the water that he had fetched.

"What am I going to do with my extra time today?" thought Jonathan. *"Maybe I could fix my bed. I have plenty of rope that I have collected over the last six months or so and the straw is ready in the fields. I will need to cut some new posts and soak the leather to bind them together."*

Jonathan knew this was no small project and it would require a lot of work. He grabbed some straw on the way back from the pond and decided to take the ax with him the next trip so he could cut the posts.

After emptying the bucket, Jonathan carried the fresh straw to the loft for his new bed. He grabbed the ax and headed for the pond. Jonathan stopped at the edge of the forest to cut a small tree that he knew would make excellent bed posts.

The sound of the ax was interrupted by a voice that played like music in the morning air. "Excuse me sir," interrupted a young woman.

For a moment Jonathan could hear nothing else. His eyes were fixed on her beauty. She had long dark hair and eyes of almonds. Her dress was gently blowing in the breeze accenting her body. "Sir, may I possibly bother you for a moment?" asked the girl again.

"Sure," replied Jonathan with a voice of excitement that momentarily surprised him.

"There is a stone in my garden that is too difficult for me to remove. My mother and I are alone, and we need someone strong to help us."

Jonathan immediately offered his help and followed the young lady a short distance to her home.

She abruptly and somewhat awkwardly broke the silence, "My name is Heather, and what is yours?"

"Jonathan," he stated with a little extra power in his voice.

"Well Jonathan, here is the rock. Do you think you can help?" she asked.

"Of course, I can," replied Jonathan as he reached down to test the size. Jonathan dug around the rock for a few moments before realizing that this was going to take more than a few minutes. In a way this pleased Jonathan because he would not need to find an excuse to see Heather again. "I will be back later with the proper tools," said Jonathan.

Heather thanked Jonathan as he headed across the field to gather his bucket, ax, and the tree that he had cut down. He then headed back to the stable. Even though the tree was only a few inches in diameter, it was quite long, and Jonathan was tired when he arrived at the stable.

During his short lunch, Jonathan cut the tree into four pieces to make the bed posts. He then realized he needed more trees to make the frame, so after lunch Jonathan placed a spade and the ax into his pack. On the way to the pond Jonathan stopped by Heather's house to dig out the rock.

Heather was happy to see him return so soon and greeted him with a warm smile that made Jonathan blush. Jonathan laid down his pack and took out the spade to dig out the rock. Heather saw the book and asked Jonathan, "Do you know how to read?"

"Yes," replied Jonathan. "I learned when I was very young."

"That is very unusual, I also learned when I was young," replied Heather. "Do you mind if I read the story?"

Jonathan was uneasy. Heather was very attractive, but he did not know her.

"Come on!" she smiled. "You know where I live, and besides, I know you will come back if I have the book."

Jonathan was charmed and before he could say no, she giggled and sat down to look at the book. Jonathan thought it would not matter anyway, especially since she did not know the book was supposed to be something special. Jonathan dug around the rock for a little while always watching Heather as she looked at the book.

"Run along," said Heather. "You have chores you need to do. The book will be safe with me. I promise. Come back to finish this when you have time."

Jonathan smiled nervously and reluctantly took his ax and bucket. He dropped the ax by a tree and fetched another bucket of water. On the way back he cut down another tree and walked by Heather's house. "Do you mind if I leave my ax here until I return so I do not need to carry it back and forth?" asked Jonathan.

Heather nodded her head and gave no verbal reply to Jonathan. He proceeded back to the stable all the time wondering, *what could take her so long to read the book. There were only a few pages, and she should have been done long ago.* Jonathan worried that she may know more than what he gave her credit for. He emptied the bucket, dropped the tree, and hurried back toward the pond.

"Back so fast?" asked Heather.

"Have you finished the book?" asked Jonathan as he picked up the ax.

"If you don't mind," said Heather shyly. "I would like to read this a little longer while you finish your chores."

Jonathan shook his head with a quick sign of acknowledgment and continued to the pond. In no time Jonathan had cut another tree, filled the bucket with water and returned to Heather.

Before Jonathan had time to say anything, Heather asked, "Would you like to stop by for dinner tonight?"

Jonathan was caught off guard and replied yes without thought. He wanted to see Heather again and was halfway back to the stable before he realized he had left the book.

For a moment Jonathan wondered if Heather knew the witches or even worse, maybe she was one of the witches in disguise. He quickly brushed the thought aside. Jonathan decided the evening was early enough to get the book back and besides he was sure she would return the book.

Jonathan finished the work around the stable and then cut the two trees into four pieces to make the bed frame. He tied the bed together with the leather and wove the remainder of the rope to make a mattress support. Finally, he placed the straw on the bed. Jonathan lay down on the bed and decided he would need to make a few more trips to get enough straw to make the bed soft. In the act of resting, he was startled by Smokey pouncing on a mouse.

"I wonder if that cat waited all day for that mouse?" thought Jonathan. He thought about all the work of the day to make the bed and to start digging the rock. He realized that to accomplish anything of importance required lots of effort. "Once again the book was right," he exclaimed. "The wind represented the effort needed before the sand could be blown away and constant effort must be applied for success."

Chapter 7
Summary One

Jonathan jumped out of the bed, washed his hands, and ran to Heather's house. He knew he would enjoy the dinner no matter what she cooked. Jonathan stopped just before reaching the door. He could see Heather through the window, and he was captured by her beauty in the candlelight. He paused a few moments to catch his breath then knocked on the door. As she opened the door a gentle breeze brushed her hair across her face. Jonathan was sure she was a princess for no one could be as stunning.

"Ah, Jonathan, I am glad that you came. It was getting a little late and I thought you might have been detained."

"No," replied Jonathan. "It is just that I have had a lot on my mind lately."

"The book?" she questioned.

"Yes, as a matter of fact the book has been on my mind," answered Jonathan.

"Mine too," she said. Jonathan's eyes caught Heather's and they stared in silence for a few moments. "Tell me about the book. Where did you get it? Is it really the key to success?" asked Heather. "I am sorry, please come in. This is my mother Mrs. Becket."

"Good evening Mrs. Becket," acknowledged Jonathan.

"My father recently died from the plague while in the service of the King. We had not seen him in over six months before we found out. Communication is always difficult," said Heather.

"I am sorry," replied Jonathan. He could see the sorrow in her eyes as her mother turned silently back to the stove.

"Please come sit down. I would really like to hear the story of the book," stated Heather with a twinkle returning to her eyes and a smile on her face. "I believe there is magic in the book, not just a fairy tale of poems."

Jonathan told her about finding the book in the forest and the three witches that banished the old man.

"The book says all you need is a better understanding. Have you found any truths to what you have read?" questioned Heather.

"We can talk as we eat," replied Mrs. Becket as she placed various items on the table.

Heather was mixing a drink as she spoke. She placed it on the table with the other items. Heather and her mother sat down and after a short blessing Mrs. Becket nodded toward the food and said, "Please eat, it has been a long time since a man has sampled our food."

Jonathan was delighted with everything he ate as he knew he would. "What is this drink you have prepared Heather? It is delicious."

"It is a little something I mixed together from the common fruits and vegetables out of my garden. I was experimenting one day, and I guess it turned out okay because everyone seems to like it." she said.

"I have never tasted anything quite like it before," replied Jonathan. He was truly impressed with the drink, not just trying to be polite.

"So, tell me. What have you learned about the book?" questioned Heather one more time.

"Well," said Jonathan. "I learned that I could be what I want to be. I must not let others tell me what they think I am, or I may believe them and become what they expect me to be. I must not dwell on the problems of the past or they will affect my future. I must take care what I believe because that is what I become. Leadership is taking the initiative. People will do what you want them to if you guide them in your direction. Otherwise, you will be a follower and do what they want done if you let them guide you. You must have a plan. If you do not plan, your greatest ideas will only remain as ideas or be covered with other ideas. You must dream. Stretch your imagination and reach for the stars. Do not let beliefs limit what you can obtain; rather let your beliefs obtain the limits of your imagination. Finally, I must put forth the effort and work before anything will come to me. Nothing is free."

"Wow, the book says all that!" exclaimed Heather.

"Amazing as it may seem that is only in the first few chapters." said Jonathan with a sly smile on his face.

Chapter 8
Harmony

"Show me where you are in the book Jonathan?" said Heather impulsively.

Jonathan turned a few pages and opened the book to the next chapter. Together, they read the next two lines.

"IT TAKES TWO BIRDS IN HARMONY BEFORE THE NEST IS DONE. A FLOCK OF BIRDS FLYING BY CAN MAKE THE TIGER RUN."

"I know what the first sentence means!" said Heather excitedly.

Jonathan looked at her with doubt and quietly encouraged her to speak.

"Don't you see Jonathan; you need a partner. Everyone needs someone to support them and help them achieve success. It was no mistake that you found me, and I found you. If you want my help Jonathan, I will help you find the secret to success."

Jonathan liked the idea of someone talking to about the book. No one else seemed to be of help. In fact, everyone else discouraged him. "Okay!" said Jonathan. "What do you think the second sentence means?"

"I do not know," replied Heather. "I have seen very small birds frighten large animals when they fly all at once."

It was late and Jonathan was tired. He excused himself, picked up the book and headed back to the stable. On the way back he picked up another load of straw for his bed. The bed felt good tonight and Jonathan was proud of the work performed in one day.

As he started to doze off, he thought of Heather's drink, *"I bet we could sell her drink at the fair and if enough people heard about it during the busy season, we may be able to sell it all over the kingdom. This may be the beginning of my success and I could not think of anyone else that would make a better partner."* Jonathan was soon dreaming in the crisp evening air.

Morning came quickly and Jonathan was up like a shot. He threw new hay to the horses and cleaned the stable. He grabbed his bucket and headed for the pond. On the way to the pond, he saw Heather working in her garden.

"Good morning, Heather," said Jonathan. "I did not expect to see you so early."

"I do not usually get up this early, but I had an idea last night. Do you really think my drink is better than average?" questioned Heather.

"Of course, it is and that reminds me," started Jonathan.

"What if we sell the drink at the fair?" joined Heather in complete harmony with

Jonathan. They both laughed because they had said the same thing at the same time.

"Can you believe that we both dreamed of vegetables all night!" exclaimed Jonathan.

She was still laughing as Jonathan headed to the pond.

"First I must remove the rock from her garden," thought Jonathan. *"It is far too heavy for me so I will try to borrow Jeffrey and Michael for the task."*

Jonathan stopped by the beverage stand and asked Michael if he would be available sometime during the day. Michael was more than willing to help an old friend.

"I will keep my schedule open," said Michael.

"How about just before lunch?" asked Jonathan.

"I will be there, and I will pick up Jeffrey on the way. You can count on us," said Michael.

The morning chores passed quickly, and Jonathan arrived at Heather's house just before noon. Jeffrey and Michael were only a short distance down the path.

"Good afternoon. We missed you at the fairground yesterday," said Jeffrey. "We thought you were going to watch the knights practice?"

"I was a little tied up fixing my bed," replied Jonathan. He was too shy to mention he was at Heather's for dinner and had forgotten his friends.

The rock was almost four feet in diameter, and it took a lot of thinking and effort to move it from the hole. Soon the boys had accomplished the job and rolled it a few feet to the front of the garden.

"Look at this?" said Jonathan. "There is a big hole in this rock that looks like a storage shelf and the top is perfectly flat!"

Heather approached the boys to find out why Jonathan was so excited.

"We don't even have to move the rock, Heather. We can use the rock as a beverage stand. There is a tabletop to serve the drinks and a place to store the mix," continued Jonathan.

Heather was pleased and nodded her acknowledgment to Jonathan about his idea. "The rock is now just at the edge of the road to town and with a little imagination I think I can make it attractive enough to catch a few customers," injected Heather.

"What beverage stand?" asked Michael.

"What drink?" added Jeffrey.

"You guys could use a little refreshment after the work you just performed. Heather, do you have a couple drinks for some hard-working men?" asked Jonathan.

Heather departed without a word and returned with a pitcher of her special mixture. She poured some for each of the boys and waited for their reaction. The response was instantaneous and positive.

"This is what you want to sell?" questioned Jeffrey. "It really is good."

"You are going to need more than a pitcher of this. I know people will want this and I can speak from experience," said Michael.

Jonathan was pleased but the guys had brought up a good point. They were going to need a lot of ingredients if the word got around. "How hard is it to make this Heather?" asked Jonathan.

"Not hard. Mostly water and a special mixture of several common items that grow all over the valley. The secret is to prepare the drink with the correct proportions, or the drink will be too bitter, too sweet, or not any good at all." answered Heather.

"We will need to make arrangements to secure all the necessary ingredients in the event that many people want the drink," interrupted Michael.

"You are right Michael, but we must all get back to our normal chores or our bosses will run us out of the kingdom. Thank you for the help," said Jonathan. The three boys started off on their separate ways.

"Oh, Jonathan," called Heather. "Do you know what the second part of the riddle is?"

Jonathan stopped, looked back, and shook his head no.

"You can do greater things with the help of many than what you could ever do by yourself," she replied.

Jonathan thought about the help he needed to move the rock and the ideas generated by many people to set up the stand. *"It was true that a person needs a close partner for personal support, and it is necessary to have a team for real success,"* thought Jonathan. It really was true, any group of individuals as a team could perform far beyond the capability of each one independently.

Chapter 9
Your Own

"Michael, Jeffrey, come on back," called Mrs. Becket as she brought out sandwiches for the three young men, dusted off the new beverage tabletop, laid the small lunch down and asked the three to join them.

"How come everyone is talking about riddles?" asked Michael.

"Yeah," said Jeffrey. "Riddles and stories, books, fame and fortune.... will someone please tell me what is going on?"

Jonathan told the two boys the story of finding the book and the solution to several riddles.

"Where is this book, Jonathan?" asked Michael.

Heather looked at Jonathan for permission as she took the small book from his pack.

"It sure doesn't look like much," said Jeffrey as he inspected the small leather-bound book.

The book was handsome, printed with gold lettering and definitely made with care.

Jeffrey opened the book and immediately started to laugh, "How could you take something like this seriously, Jonathan?

There are only a few sentences in this thing. I think someone gave you a little too much to drink the other night."

"No!" shouted Jonathan. "I did not believe it either, but it is true."

"Okay," injected Michael. "How about reading us a magic chapter?"

Jonathan opened the book to the next chapter and read aloud.

"LOOK AT THINGS AROUND YOU ON YOUR WAY HOME, ALL THINGS OF GREATNESS COME FROM YOUR OWN."

"That's it?" asked Michael with a puzzled look on his face. "What is it supposed to mean? Lots of things are great and I didn't make any of them."

"I do not know," said Jonathan. "But this book has a magic way of showing me the answer before the end of the day."

"How could something so simple be so important that witches thought they needed the book?" questioned Jeffrey.

"Well, what do you think this parable means?" asked Jonathan of his three companions.

No one answered and they all shrugged their shoulders in response.

Jonathan thanked Heather for the lunch, placed the book into his pack, grabbed his bucket and bid good-bye to his friends as he started back to the pond. Jonathan thought quietly about the mill as he walked toward the pond, *Someday I hope to have a small business like that. The miller has truly done a great job of keeping the mill running.*

Jonathan could see Michael in the distance approaching the beverage stand. *I wonder if Michael will ever own his own business. He has worked for just about everybody in the village. He is such a hard worker and a pleasant person to be around. He should have his own beverage stand by now.*

Further down the path Jonathan noticed the court jester on his way back to the castle from his own lunch. "The jester has a beautiful home, why is he more successful than Michael or me for that matter? After all I still sleep in the stable. I do not even have a small room," muttered Jonathan.

Jonathan's thoughts were interrupted. "Would you like to buy some bread?" asked the young girl Teresa.

"Sure," said Jonathan as he gave her a half-penny for a large loaf.

Jonathan went back into thought; *this young girl was ambitious. In the last year she paid for a new cart for her father from the earnings she made reselling bread from the bakery.*

The stable appeared to grow in size as Jonathan approached. The Baron was just leaving on his horse and his silhouette made him appear as large as the stable.

 shouted Jonathan. The Baron's horse jumped slightly at the sudden noise. "Success comes from owning your own business. The jester, the young girl, the miller, and the Baron all own their own business. Michael and I work hard but we will never have major success unless we work for ourselves. What a stroke of good luck finding Heather just in time to start a business of my own."

Jonathan was so lost in excitement that he almost forgot to empty the bucket. He returned to the trough and dumped the bucket.

Jonathan was whistling on his way to the pond and did not see Heather standing by the rock. "What do you think?" asked Heather confidently as she pointed to the rock.

Jonathan was impressed. If you did not know it was a rock, you would not recognize it. She had tied a light blanket to several trees to provide shade. Four stumps had been placed in front of the rock as chairs and the rock was shining like silver.

"I had Jeffrey place the stumps for me. Come look at the back. It was easy for me to clean up the rock and my first drink is prepared," added Heather proudly. "Sit and have a drink," she begged.

Jonathan placed a quarter penny on the counter.

Heather smiled at him and said, "a farthing it tis." She placed the small coin in another small hole in the rock. "May this be the first of many profits," she said as she toasted Jonathan.

Several small birds flew into the air at the sound of their mugs clashing. "I found the answer Heather. The beverage stand is ours and it is necessary for success," said Jonathan.

"Really?" questioned Heather. "I know many people that are successful, and they do not have a beverage stand."

"No Heather," added Jonathan. "The riddle only means that to obtain financial success you must have your own business."

"I can understand that" continued Heather. She sat down on the old tree and patted the place beside her. "So, what is the next riddle?"

Chapter 10
The Path

They opened the book together and read,

"THE PATH MAY APPEAR SMOOTH AND TOUGH BUT TO AN ANT IT IS SIGNIFICANTLY LOOSE AND ROUGH."

"That is sure true!" said Jonathan. "When I walk down the path it is smooth and hard to me, but could you imagine if you were an ant? Every little piece of sand would look like the rock we made the beverage stand from. The whole road would be movable to the ant."

"That is true Jonathan, but I really think there must be more to the riddle than that," interrupted Heather.

"Hey you two!" shouted Jeffrey. "How you going to get rich sitting like two bumps on a log?" His cliché was very appropriate considering they were sitting on a log.

"We are making plans for our business," replied Jonathan.

"Well, you better make lots of them so that one of them might work. No offense Heather but I do not think carrot juice will make you rich," laughed Jeffrey as he continued down the path.

Before Jonathan could say anything, the Baron appeared. Jonathan was startled that he had not seen him arrive. The Baron dismounted the horse and sat down. "I hear you have quite a drink young lady. May I have some?" asked the Baron.

"Sure." replied Heather timidly as she handed him a mug.

The Baron did not say much as he drank the drink and Jonathan was a little nervous having his boss see him sitting down.

"That was excellent Heather, and you are working with a smart young man," commented the Baron as he rose to leave. "You always do twice the work of the other stable boys Jonathan and you still have the ambition to better yourself. The word is already getting around about this drink. You might have something big here. It was good enough for me to want to come back again sometime soon. I will tell others about your special brew."

The Baron placed a penny on the counter and started to mount his horse. "Sir," intruded Jonathan. "The drink is only a farthing."

"Honesty too!" said the Baron. "Keep the change. I have paid much more for far less."

As the Baron rode away Jonathan looked at Heather in disbelief. "Have you had any customers yet?" questioned Jonathan.

"Nay," said Heather with equal amazement. "I have only told a few friends, but none have come since we opened."

"I too," replied Jonathan. "Only a few friends like Jeffrey and Michael."

Jonathan excused himself and ran to the pond. He did not want to disappoint the Baron.

"Well, if it isn't the new tavern owner," called the storyteller. "I have seen many try to sell snake oil and none have succeeded."

"I am not selling snake oil and I will succeed." snapped Jonathan.

"Aye lad," interrupted the beggar. "Maybe you will succeed but it will not be easy."

"Easy!" continued the storyteller. "He has no experience and is just a stable boy. I tried to sell a potion of my own once and it never got off the ground. Take my advice boy and get back to the stable while you still have a job."

Jonathan thanked them for their advice and continued quickly back to the stable. On the way back to the stable Jonathan encountered the young baker girl.

"I wish you were my partner, Jonathan. A beverage stand would be much easier than traveling the countryside selling bread," she cooed.

Jonathan tipped his hat and continued on without a word. He continued his daily chores lost in thought. Jonathan made several trips to the pond and cleaned the stable unconsciously during the day. The day was over, and he was tired as he lay in bed thinking about the riddle. He was sure he had the meaning of the last riddle as he slowly started to doze off to sleep.

"Some people will think anything you do is hard, and others will think everything is easy," Jonathan thought. *"Other people will see what I must do differently than I do. In order for me to understand their comments and not be discouraged, I must realize they see the world differently than I do. I must walk on the path and not in the path if I am to move ahead quickly."* Jonathan fell asleep with a feeling of confidence and peace.

Chapter 11
Time

Jonathan woke up refreshed and ready for another day. He smiled with a deeper understanding as he opened the pack. Jonathan was amazed at how much he had learned from just a few lines. To know that a power much more magical than a few spells a witch could perform was in his hands made him far more confident. Jonathan opened the book and read the next few lines.

"STOP THE CLOCK, NO MATTER HOW HARD YOU TRY, TIME KEEPS ON MOVING IT WILL PASS YOU BY. BUT FROM THIS LESSON IF YOU BELIEVE, YOUR GREATEST RICHES WILL BE CONCEIVED."

Jonathan had heard about a clock. The Tinkerer in town had one even though Jonathan had never seen one before.

Jonathan had been working pretty hard the last few days and he decided to take a little visit to the castle. Maybe he could find an answer to the riddle from the Tinkerer. Jonathan made several trips for water faster than normal and then headed for the castle. He stopped by to see Heather on the way and was surprised to find all four seats taken at the beverage stand.

"Jonathan, I need to talk to you right away," said Heather as she pulled him by the arm to the side of the garden. "I need several items from town. I have sold all my mixture three times already this morning. Some travelers are asking me to prepare some for their trip back home and I need something to put the drink into. I need some leather flasks and several items in the garden are sure to run out soon. We have made a very good profit but not enough to pay for flasks. Maybe the store will take credit until the flasks are sold."

She gave him the money and Jonathan headed to town with another mission added to his list of things to do. At the entrance to town the architect was drawing plans for a new castle gate. Jonathan was impressed and asked the man how he could build a castle of such magnitude.

"One brick at a time," smiled the architect as he continued on with his work.

The first shop that Jonathan visited was the Tinker Shop. "Excuse me sir, do you have a clock?" The old man looked over the top of his spectacles to see this young curious man.

"As a matter of fact, I do have a clock." replied the man.

"What is it used for?" asked Jonathan.

"It is used to tell you the time. See it is now ten fifteen." answered the old man.

"Well what good is it? What is ten fifteen?" questioned Jonathan.

The old man started, "Suppose you and a friend wanted to meet at a certain time, like practicing archery. If you agreed to meet at ten fifteen, then both of you would be at the same place at the same time if you had a clock."

"Very interesting," said Jonathan, "but I can tell the time by the sun and this clock is too big to carry every time I want to know the time. Besides two people would need a clock to be of any use."

"That is true," replied the man, "but someday everyone will have a clock!"

"Very interesting but what if my clock breaks and I do not know the time for archery?" asked Jonathan.

"Aha, then you will miss your game because the time will still come even without the clock," smiled the Tinkerer.

"Thank you, sir, for sharing your time and the invention. "Someday maybe even I will have need for a clock," replied Jonathan as he exited to the morning streets.

Jonathan entered the dry goods store to see if the proprietor had any flasks.

"May I help you sir?" asked mister Applebee the owner.

Jonathan was not accustomed to being called sir and it took him a moment to realize the owner had addressed him. "I am sorry sir; I must have been dreaming.

Do you have any leather flasks?" answered Jonathan.

"What are you going to put in them?" asked the man.

"Some drinks for travelers, sir," replied Jonathan. "We have a beverage stand and people want to take the drink with them."

"You must be young Jonathan, the one tied up with Heather on a new business venture," continued the man. "I heard all about it. In fact, I bet everyone in town knows about your business already. You don't need a flask son; you need a bottle."

"What is a bottle?" questioned Jonathan.

"A new great idea made out of glass. It is cheap and it is easy to clean, perfect for your needs," replied the proprietor.

"I only have forty-six pennies; how many can I buy?" asked Jonathan.

"Only forty-six pennies!" laughed the owner. "Some people don't make that much money in a month, and you want to spend it all on bottles. Let me tell you son, buy only a few now and build your inventory, as you need it. More importantly you better use your money to secure the ingredients for your brew. From the talk in town, every farmer in the valley is making preparations to sell you materials for the fair during the next few weeks."

Jonathan purchased several different bottles and some wax to seal the ends. The price was right, and he was wondering if he could bottle the drink for shipping to other towns after the fair was over. That thought passed quickly after remembering barrels would work much better.

Jonathan picked up a few items for Heather on his way back. He now knew the answer to the riddle, and he spoke it aloud to himself, "Time is precious and will wait for no one, but like the castle being built one brick at a time, anything can be done if you just keep working. I must now make out a plan like the book said in the very beginning and work at it every day."

Jonathan arrived at the stand to see Heather sitting alone. "Is there anything wrong?" asked Jonathan.

"Oh no," replied Heather with a weary voice. "It is just that I have not been able to stop all day. This is the first time I have not had customers."

"I discovered another riddle, Heather. I think it is time that I help you with the business, at least during the next few weeks. I know they need me at the stable because of the fair but someone else can do the job. I can return to the stable after the fair."

A sigh of relief overcame Heather. The beverage stand was too much for her to handle by herself. "Why don't you get your things and stay in the shed?" asked Heather shyly, "It really is in very good condition. I am beginning to like this book even better if it told you, it was time to help."

"Well, that is not exactly what it said but it did say that I better stick to what I started," replied Jonathan. "I will go get my bed and a few other things right away."

Chapter 12
Team

"What is the next riddle, Jonathan?" asked Heather.

Jonathan opened the book and gave it to Heather. She read the following lines,

"ONE FISH ALONE COULD NOT FEED ITSELF, BUT THOUSANDS TOGETHER PUT FOOD ON YOUR SHELF."

Jonathan laughed, "All fish feed themselves, unless the riddle means the fish is going to eat itself! I guess it means you need a lot of fish before you have enough."

I don't think so Jonathan," said Heather. "Go get your belongings, we have a lot to do."

Jonathan approached the stable with a little remorse. He was not sure he was doing the right thing by quitting his job, but he really was not happy working at something that had no future.

"Just what I expected!" said the stable master when he saw Jonathan gathering his things. "If I have my way you will never work here again. For that matter I will do my best to ensure you do not work for anyone. After your head heals come back and talk to me. Maybe I will let you start back at the bottom where you were three years ago."

Jonathan was not sure he was doing the right thing. After all he had a good job with a place to stay. He had plenty of food and a little spending money. *"What more should I ask for?"* thought Jonathan. *"Well, I can get a job anyplace if I want to and this new venture is business working for myself."* The thought sounded good to Jonathan, making him feel a little bit more secure in his decision.

"Leaving already?" asked the Baron. Jonathan was startled by the Baron's voice. He had been doing a lot of daydreaming lately and missed the Baron's appearance completely.

"Aah," started Jonathan showing a lot of embarrassment. "I need to help Heather with the beverage stand during the fair, sir. I will be back soon."

"Jonathan," interrupted the Baron. "I knew you would be gone as soon as the stable master started to tell me about your ideas and excitement for success. If you need a job, I will be happy to have you back, but I believe you will find your success. If not at the beverage stand then your success will come elsewhere."

Jonathan smiled timidly at the Baron and continued back to the stand.

"Jonathan, I need some onions and celery," called Heather as soon as Jonathan was in earshot. "The garden is completely out, and I believe the Jenkens down the road have plenty. Could you see if they will sell you some?"

Jonathan placed his belongings in the shed, grabbed a small basket and picked up some money for the purchase. He would need to get his other belongings later that day.

"Jonathan, will you please deliver these bottles to Michael at his beverage stand? He has been selling some of the product for me. Also, we need some more bottles from town," smiled Heather. She knew a sweet touch might ease the burden of work.

Jonathan returned a smile to her and headed to the Jenkens'.

"Excuse me Mrs. Jenkens," asked Jonathan politely. "Could I purchase some onions and celery?"

"I would be delighted to help you Jonathan," she replied. "I expected you sooner than this. You will sure make my job easier if you purchase my products. Everyone is wondering how much you can sell. I tried the drink myself and it was delicious. I will be buying some for my family, and I am sure they will enjoy it."

Jonathan thanked Mrs. Jenkens, loaded the vegetables into his basket and headed back to the stand. He unloaded the basket, waved good-bye to Heather and headed to town for the bottles. On his way he dropped off the product for Michael.

"Good afternoon, Jonathan," said the storekeeper. "I hear business is really booming for you. Everyone is talking about your drink, and I would like you to bring me some the next time you pass my way."

"I would be happy to Mr. Applebee," replied Jonathan.

"Hey, Jonathan," called a voice from outside. "I have been trying to catch you all day."

Jonathan turned to see the person attached to the voice. It was Christopher, a young farmer from the other side of town.

"I have a business proposition for you. I must have had a hundred people come by my vegetable stand today and ask if I was selling your drink. How about if I buy your product and sell it to the travelers on the other side of town? I heard that Michael is already selling some for you too and this will add customers that you would not normally contact." said Christopher.

The idea appealed to Jonathan. "How many bottles would you want to start with?" asked Jonathan.

"I was thinking more like a barrel to start and then we could figure out the volume needed over the next few days. I expect I may need a barrel a day when the fair starts up." said Christopher.

Jonathan did not know what to say. He was completely caught off guard. "Do you have a barrel?" asked Jonathan. He was still in a daze.

"I will have my hired hand bring one right over." replied Christopher.

Jonathan quickly came to his senses and realized that Heather probably did not have a barrel of product made up. In fact, it would probably take most of the day to finish just what was needed for his beverage stand. Also, the raw materials were already short in Heather's garden.

"We need to talk this over Christopher," said Jonathan with more confidence. "I will give you a list of items needed, and I will need the help of your hired hand for an hour to prepare the mixture. We can work out the details of payment and the credit for your raw materials. I will need to hire some people to produce and deliver the drink and someone is going to need to secure the necessary raw materials."

"This business could be fun!" added Mr. Applebee. "I will rent you a couple barrels for a few weeks during the fair and you can purchase them in a few weeks if you want when your profits are higher. Also, you will need a lot of bottles. I will sell them to you at a good price and give you a week to pay."

Jonathan was pleased with the help he was receiving from everyone, but he also knew that his business meant profit for everyone else. Jonathan knew he must make plans to keep his business alive after the fair.

He barely heard Mr. Applebee call out in the distance, "Put a name on that stuff son, no one knows what to ask for and I cannot keep saying it is the magic brew. We all know that only wizards and witches and other magic people can have success the easy way."

Jonathan could still hear the laughter of Mr. Applebee in his mind when he sat down exhausted at the beverage stand from carrying all the bottles.

Jeffrey approached and sat down by Jonathan. "Could I have a drink, Heather?" asked Jeffrey.

Before Jeffrey had a chance to taste the drink, Jonathan asked, "How would you like to make a few extra pennies Jeffrey?"

Jeffrey nodded his head yes as he took a large swallow of the mixture.

"I need someone to inventory the products in the valley needed for the drink. At least I need to have an idea of how much brew we might be able to make," added Jonathan.

Heather interrupted with a sharp voice, "I do not appreciate my drink being referred to as a brew. You know they burn witches, and my drink is good for you. I am not a witch."

"I am sorry Heather," apologized Jonathan. "You are far too beautiful to be a witch. We do need to come up with a name though."

A smile returned to Heather's face as she accepted Jonathan's apology and compliment.

"How about Vegetable Fair for a name?" said Jeffrey.

"Sounds okay to me," replied Heather.

"I don't like it," said Jonathan, "but any name is all right for now. Vegetable Fair it shall be."

"It has more than vegetables in it," said Heather. "In fact, I even add a little of my apple wine."

"No wonder I want to drink this all day," laughed Jeffrey.

"There is not that much wine in it!" added Heather.

Jeffrey and Heather continued to talk back and forth while Jonathan was lost in thought again. When he finally returned to the conversation he said, "I know the answer to the last riddle. A business by itself will hardly pay for itself. You must duplicate your effort to become really successful. Now that Michael and Christopher are selling the product, Jeffrey is helping me find raw materials and everyone is preparing to sell necessary items to us, we can become much more successful than if we tried to do the business only by ourselves."

"What else does the book say Jonathan?" asked Jeffrey.

"Yes," added Heather. "What have you learned the last couple days?"

"Well," said Jonathan. "Since we first talked the other night, I have learned that you must have a close partner to support you when others try to put you down. A team of people working together can accomplish anything. You must be in business for yourself to accomplish financial success. A job will give you security and it is necessary while you grow but it must be put aside for true success. Many people will try to discourage you. They will look at the immediate problems and tell you it cannot be done. You must overcome the problems and not let them overcome you. Time is your partner and not your enemy as long as you know time will overcome any obstacle. You must keep up a constant effort. Finally, as I just said, you must duplicate your effort. Other people must do what you do to truly become success ful. A little profit from many people can be far greater than all you can produce with your own work."

Jeffrey looked at Jonathan with amazement and said, "I read that book and I never saw anything that you said in the pages I read."

"I did," interrupted Heather. "Everything you said is true and I read the same as you Jonathan!"

Jonathan broke the silence by asking Jeffrey to help him carry his bed back to the shed.

"Sure," said Jeffrey still in a light trance, "but could we read the next chapter again just for fun?"

Jonathan smiled and opened the book. All three looked with intense interest as Jonathan read,

"AN UNLIT CANDLE SHEDS A DIFFERENT LIGHT FOR TWO

SEPARATE PEOPLE ON THE SAME DARK NIGHT."

"Wow," said Jeffrey. "I am confused even more. How can an unlit candle shed any light at all for anyone?"

"I don't know," said Heather, "but why don't you come back tonight, and we can have some fun trying to find out?"

Jeffrey agreed and said he would get Michael and meet them just after dark.

At this point both Jonathan and Jeffrey headed toward the stable to get Jonathan's bed. They had dismantled the bed, took the last of Jonathan's belongings and were on the way back to Heather's house when Jonathan remembered that Christopher was going to send the hired hand to get some Vegetable Fair.

"We must hurry," said Jonathan. "I need to make a large batch of product for our new partner. When we get back, Jeffrey, I need you to pick up some items from the local farmers so that we have enough raw goods."

"I will help as much as possible, but I need to finish my work at the mill also," replied Jeffrey.

When they arrived at Heather's house, they found Heather busy mixing a large batch of product right in the barrel. Several customers were at the stand, and no one was available to wait on them. Heather did not look very happy when they arrived. "Why didn't you tell me that someone was going to come by to pick up a large barrel of product? I would have told you to stay and get your belongings later," scolded Heather.

"I am sorry Heather, I forgot they were coming. Things are happening so fast," apologized Jonathan.

Jonathan took over the mixing from Heather and let her attend to the customers at the stand. Within an hour Jonathan had finished his work and gave the full barrel to Christopher's hired hand.

"I left a barrel for you by the shed," said the helper. "Christopher said you could probably use it and he could always get it later when he needs another barrel of product."

"Thank you very much," replied Jonathan. "We can use the barrel to store product for Heather while I am attending to other business."

"We need to pay attention to the stand Jonathan," said Heather. We can always make plans for partners later on. I am going to need lots of vegetables, and you need to mix them for me because you are stronger."

Jonathan mixed another barrel of product over the next two hours. The barrel was larger than the one he sent to Christopher, but it was worth the effort knowing that tomorrow would be a free day to catch up on business. "Tomorrow I will go to town and see about selling bottles in the shops," said Jonathan.

"Tomorrow, I need you to help me arrange the beverage stand and make plans for the fair customers," replied Heather. "We will be plenty busy with the out-of-town people. Besides it is important that we spread the word by our customers so that we can sell products after the fair."

Jonathan acknowledged that he needed to help Heather get things started at home first.

The remainder of the day passed quickly and shortly after eating both Jeffrey and Michael arrived for an evening of social activity. They talked for over an hour by candlelight when Heather suggested, "Why don't we try to solve the riddle?"

"What riddle?" asked Michael.

They explained the riddle to Michael, then Heather blew out the candle and the four of them sat in the dark. "We now have an unlit candle," said Heather. "What do you see?"

"I don't see anything," said Jeffrey sarcastically. "How can you see in the dark?"

"I can see in the dark," said Michael. "I can see the three of you, the candle, the table and the outline of the trees against the sky."

"Aah ha!" said Jonathan. "I can see the shed, the house, and the path in the light of the unlit candle. What do you see Heather."

"Oh, I see what you see and much more," replied Heather. "I can see the stream and the fish swimming, I can see the castle and the children playing, I can hear the birds and see the trees blowing gently in the breeze."

"Surely you are joking Heather?" questioned Jeffrey. "It is dark out; the children are sleeping, and the wind is not blowing.

"That is true Jeffrey," answered Heather. "But nevertheless, I can see all that in my mind, even with the unlit candle."

All three boys sat in silence, and they realized it was true.

"So, what does the riddle mean?" asked Michael.

Heather and Jonathan looked at each other and smiled. "I want to prepare the business for partners," said Jonathan.

"I want to ensure the business works good as a beverage stand with future customers," added Heather.

"We both want to carry our business throughout the kingdom, but we have different ideas on how to do the business," continued Jonathan.

"Though we both have the same desire for success, each of us has different goals. We must understand that we each have a different perspective about what we want from our success," finished Heather.

"You must work together to obtain the maximum benefit from each other's ideas," added Michael with a proud sense of understanding.

Chapter 14
Belief

Before departing for the evening Jonathan opened the book to read the next chapter from "The Key to Success". His three friends sat quietly as Jonathan read,

"IF YOU KNOW THE WISH IS TRUE, YOU CAN EXPECT THE BEST FOR YOU."

"That will give me a lot to think about," said Michael. "How can a wish be true until it happens? It is not a wish if it is true. My wish is to own a beverage stand instead of just working in one. I have had the same wish for five years. It is not true, but it is my wish."

"None of my wishes ever come true," said Jeffrey.

"My wish is success!" said Jonathan.

"You better be a little more specific Jonathan," said Heather. "I wish I had curtains for my windows. Bright shinny curtains with lace on the bottom."

Jeffrey and Michael bid good night and headed for home. Heather went inside her house, and Jonathan retired to the shed. All four wondered what the meaning of this new riddle could be.

Jonathan woke up in the morning with a feeling much different than he had ever had in the past. He felt a strange feeling of security as he listened to the birds chirping in the early morning outside the small shed. He decided this is the feeling one gets when you own your own life and have control of yourself. Just the idea that no one was going to yell at him to get up, except maybe his customers, made him feel good.

Even though the shed was small, it was a place he could almost call his own and it made him proud. He knew it would not be long before he would have a place of his own. Jonathan had never really thought about it, but he had planned on having his own place someday. As soon as he had started the business, a place to stay had entered his mind. He needed to think of what he wanted including a place to live. *"Maybe that is what the book meant. I need to expect a little more and not just wish for what I want,"* thought Jonathan.

Jonathan started to think about Michael. Michael had a lot of dreams that he wished would come true, but he did not believe his dreams would come true. That is why he spent five years talking about his beverage stand, wishing for his beverage stand but never expecting to get his beverage stand so his dream never came true.

"Possibly this is what the riddle means," thought Jonathan. *"I will have to help Michael. I must show Michael to expect*

the beverage stand or that his dream could come true even today."

Jonathan continued to think, and he said aloud, "What about Jeffrey? He is a different kind of guy. He doesn't believe that anything will come true, he doesn't have any dreams at all whether he believed them of not!"

Jonathan continued thinking, *"I learned from the beginning of the book that I must dream a little and that is for sure. Without any dreams no one will go anyplace. Anything that has ever been done has started from a dream. Jeffrey and many people like him have no dreams. With no dreams they have no goals and therefore can have no success. Dreams are actually hope and without dreams you have no hope. Even though I have a dream, I have learned that I must dream correctly."*

Jonathan remembered the beggar, the storyteller, and the Baron. Jonathan knew he could dream too much or too little if he did not have focus. Now he had learned that he must expect the dream to come true. No matter how much you dream, like Michael does about the beverage stand, without expectation there will be no success.

Jonathan's daydreams reflected on Heather. He thought about how she seemed to get what she wanted. The beverage stand, everything around it appeared to be built to her desire. She was very specific about what she wanted, like last night when she mentioned she wanted curtains with lace on the bottom.

Possibly he could learn from this and guide his thoughts. Maybe he should take a few moments and decide what he really wanted and expected to get from his success.

Jonathan decided he wanted a house. How proud he was to have made a decision. *I want a house*, thought Jonathan. After a moment of reflection Jonathan said aloud, "No, that is not exactly what I want. I want a house. I want a painted house. I want a painted house by the stream. That is what I want."

Then Jonathan thought, *that really isn't specific either, I want to have the old home, the old cottage down by the brook that the Baron started with. I recall that cottage. I have seen it many times. The Baron occasionally uses it as a summer home now. He very seldom goes there, and it could be fixed up and made beautiful once again. Possibly the Baron would consider talking over some kind of arrangement.*

The cottage had to be in Jonathan's future, and he now expected it to be true. There was plenty of room at the cottage, he could start his business, he could store his belongings and supplies and it would be a home to be proud of.

Jonathan lay back and started to dream. He visualized the cottage with the horses coming and going pulling carts full of the Vegetable Fair product to the far reaches of the kingdom. He imagined sitting by the brook each weekend fishing and taking it easy. That is what Jonathan wanted.

Jonathan flew out of bed ready to live his dream when he stopped and said, "I think I will go to town first. I believe I owe Heather a favor."

Jonathan dressed quickly and headed for town, even before eating. On his way, as he passed the beverage stand, Michael yelled good morning to him.

"Good morning, Michael," said Jonathan. "How are you today?"

"I am fine," replied Michael. "What a lovely day it is. Where are you going Jonathan?"

"I thought I would head into town and get a little present for Heather," replied Jonathan.

"Oh, what is that?" asked Michael.

"Well, I thought I might pick up some curtains. You know, some with lace," replied Jonathan.

"Ah ha," said Michael with a short laugh. "You are going to make her wish come true."

"Well, why not, besides it is a small favor for what she has done for me," continued Jonathan.

"Hey, I don't mind going with you," said Michael. "I would like to take a few minutes off; nothing is happening here. It is too early in the morning, and I don't expect anyone for at least another hour."

"All right, come along, I would like to have company," said Jonathan.

The two of them headed for town enjoying the fresh morning air.

"By the way," said Michael. "I have been thinking. You know your beverage stands are starting to grow and I don't think you will be able to handle them all with just Heather and Christopher across town. What do you say if, ah, you get together with me? I would like to help you out. I could do quite well selling Vegetable Fair for you. You know Jonathan, I thought about it last night. I was not thinking about my beverage stand like I should. In the past I thought my wish about a beverage stand was not true, and now last night I decided that it really could be mine. There is a possibility; there is no reason why I should not have my own beverage stand. You have the belongings and product for me to help me get started. I know how to do other things such as bakeries and have the experience to make a profitable beverage stand."

Jonathan smiled, looked over at Michael and said, "You see how fast your dreams have come true? All these years, five in the past, you never expected your own beverage stand. Yet in one night you expect a beverage stand, ask for it and you get it. I had a traveler ask me one time and I never knew what he meant. He said put your hand on your shoulder."

Michael looked at Jonathan strangely.

Jonathan continued, "Yeah, Michael, put your hand on your shoulder." Michael put his hand on his shoulder and Jonathan exclaimed, "See!"

Michael questioned, "What do you mean? What does it mean?"

Jonathan added, "Well, why did you put your hand on your shoulder?"

Michael answered sarcastically, "Because you asked me to."

"Exactly!" said Jonathan. "Just like you asked me if I would give you some of my product for your beverage stand. Most people never ask for what they want. In most cases people will be glad to give us what we ask. Oh, boy, am I glad I had this talk with you! Now three wishes will be true."

"Oh," said Michael. "Why is that?"

"Well, your wish is now true. You want your own beverage stand and you will have it by the end of the day. Me, I know

and expect I will get the cottage. All I have to do is talk to the Baron and work out some kind of deal and payment plan. I believe he has faith in me, and I expect to get it and I know I will have it. And Heather – she will get her curtains."

"Aha," said Jonathan and Michael as they smiled and ran arm in arm into town. They knew many wonderful things were ahead of them.

It was early and the market was just opening. That was good because Jonathan would have a chance to find the best selection before the crowd. They walked slowly through the town looking at the various shops.

Jonathan noticed one small shop off in a corner and remembered that the lady there always had some of the nicest belonging. He stopped and looked around. In a very short time, he had found what he thought would be just what Heather wanted. The curtains had a bright yellow color to them and lace on the bottom.

He wondered how they colored the curtains. Supposedly the dies came from the orient. *Ah, the orient,* thought Jonathan. *Someday maybe I will have to go there too, but not now. I must keep my focus on the immediate task.*

As Jonathan paid for the curtains he thought about the past. It was not long ago that the money he had just paid for the curtains was more than the money he carried all month long. *How things can change when you have a goal.*

Jonathan stopped to make payments on some bottles and barrels that he owed Mr. Applebee. He asked Mr. Applebee if he could possibly have another barrel because he had a partner that was going to open a beverage stand in another part of town.

Mr. Applebee smiled and said, "I would be glad to loan you another one. Your payments are coming in faster than what they are due, and I believe we will have a good partnership for a long time."

Jonathan decided to return to the stable to rent a horse and cart to carry the barrel, bottles, and some other belongings that he needed. Besides he needed to deliver more product to Christopher across town. He needed to pick up the barrel from Christopher, mix the product and take it back to him or have his helper come over to pick up the product. Either way Jonathan knew he would need a cart for the day.

Michael decided he would help Jonathan because after all he was in business as his partner. The beverage stand Michael worked at was okay, but he was not getting paid what he felt he was worth, and it was time to move on and get his own beverage stand. Michael decided to give the owner the courtesy of knowing he was going into business for himself and stop by and inform him on the way to the stable with Jonathan. He decided to work another couple of days until he could find a replacement to run the stand.

On the way out of town the boys passed the old mill and Jeffrey greeted them, "How are you doing guys?"

"We are doing fine. We are on our way to the stable to rent a horse and cart," said Michael.

"Why are you going to do that?" said Jeffrey.

"Well," said Jonathan. "Michael and I need to pick up another barrel and start a new beverage stand."

"Oh," said Jeffrey. "Who is going to run Michael's old beverage stand?"

"That is a very good question, because Michael is going to be leaving and he will need a replacement for himself so that the owner is not left with an empty stand. How about you Jeffrey? It is a lot easier work than working at the mill and I am sure Michael's boss would like to have you working over there," said Jonathan.

"Na, not me, I don't think so. I can't make up my mind about the things that I want to do," said Jeffrey. "But my cousin Steven just got into town, and I could talk to him, maybe he would like to run the stand."

"Sure," said Michael. "Let us know what you decide."

"Okay," replied Jeffrey. "I will see you later."

"It should not be too hard to find someone to replace me," said Michael. "After all, work is not always easy to come by."

At the same time the boys approached the stable, the stable master saw them coming and laughed, smiled, and said, "How's my man? You got any STARdust in your eyes Jonathan?"

"Not too much," said Jonathan. "Things are going quite well. How are things at the stable?"

"They are doing fine," said the stable master. "You still have your job here if you decide to come back some day. Of course, your pay will only be half but that is the price you pay for fantasies," noted the stable master with a sarcastic grin.

"I am not here to look for a job," said Jonathan. "I am here to rent a horse and cart."

"Ha ha," laughed the stable master. "To rent a horse and cart takes money you know?"

"Oh yes," said Jonathan. "I understand that. I have money to rent the horse."

"Let's see it then," chided the stable master.

Jonathan slowly opened his leather pouch and took out the coins necessary for the rent of a horse and cart for the day.

"That is not enough!" huffed the stable master.

"What do you mean?" questioned Jonathan. "I have worked here for years, and I know the price of rentals. This is all that is required unless you changed your prices in the past few days."

"It is not a matter of raising the prices, I only rent to the people that I know will return my horse and cart," stated the stable master with a glare in his eyes.

"You know me," said Jonathan. "I will return the horse and cart."

"No!" said the stable master. "I don't think so, I don't believe that I need to rent to you."

Jonathan was a little discouraged and upset but Michael put his hand on Jonathan's arm and said, "Don't worry about it, there are other places to rent a horse."

The boys had hardly turned from the stable master when the Baron came walking through the door. The Baron said, "I overheard that you wanted to rent a horse and cart."

"That is right sir," said Jonathan. "I have been doing a pretty good business lately and I need to carry the materials."

"I have heard about that," injected the Baron. "I have seen the results and have tasted the fine product. You will probably become the next Baron in the county."

"I could only wish sir," said Jonathan shyly.

"We both know how things can happen, when a person starts to work on something with passion," said the Baron.

"Yes," said Jonathan. "I, I, uh guess things do start to happen when you start to think about them."

The Baron looked at the stable master and said, "I will put myself behind this boy and besides this is my stable, my horses and my carts. Rent to the lad."

Jonathan was elated and the stable master was peeved as he prepared the horse and cart. Jonathan thanked the Baron once again as he left.

"It is really amazing," thought Jonathan. "People really do want to help you if you try. Sometimes it only takes a little effort to make things really turn around."

Now that he had his horse and cart, he must start to think seriously about the things he would need, and a horse and cart was something he would probably need every day. They ought to be some of the first things on his list that he needed. Jonathan started to make plans on how he would get a horse and cart.

They arrived at the cottage shortly and Heather was standing in the garden. "Morning men; how are you today? I didn't even know you left Jonathan. I shouted out for breakfast and got no response. I thought you were just oversleeping."

"No," said Jonathan. "I had a little business to do this morning. I had to go into town and get things ready. In fact, I had to pick up another barrel for Michael. He is going to open a beverage stand on the other side of town. We don't have any business over there yet and this will allow us to cover three sides of town. I know it will not take long before we find someone to take the remaining opportunity."

Heather smiled as the boys jumped out of the cart. "How would you like to have breakfast with us Michael?" questioned Heather.

"I would not mind having a little bite since I really didn't eat too much this morning. What I did have was leftover and cold anyway," replied Michael politely.

"Come on in," said Heather.

The boys went into the house and sat down at the table. Mrs. Becket smiled and said good morning. As they prepared to eat, Jonathan laid the curtains on the table. Heather turned and saw something bright yellow folded on the table but could not quite make out what it was.

"What is that?" asked Heather.

"That is something a little special for you," replied Jonathan.

Heather crossed the room and opened the curtains and jumped with joy. She exclaimed with glee, "This is something I have always wanted!"

"You taught me last night," said Jonathan. "Not only do you need to dream but also you must expect your dreams to come true. When you went to bed last night and said specifically what kind of curtains you wanted. I could tell by the look in your eyes that you knew you would get them. You now have them and not only that Heather, but the book has also taught me a few other things. We have a horse and cart, and Michael is getting his own beverage stand. He woke up this morning expecting his own stand, he asked me for it and now he has it. Me, I know I am going to have the old cottage of the Baron's down by the mill."

They all looked at each other as they sat quietly and ate their breakfast.

"So, you must not only dream and wish," said Mrs. Becket, "but you must expect your wishes to come true." As she turned the eggs she stated, "I must think more seriously about the things I want out of life."

Jonathan smiled, Heather looked at Jonathan and all three said at the same time, "What else does the book have to say?"

Chapter 15
Difference

After completing their breakfast, the three of them went out to the shed. Jonathan dusted off the cover and opened the book and said, "Let us see what the next chapter will bring today?" he read,

"THE DIFFERENCE BETWEEN THE TOP OF THE BREAD AND THE BOTTOM FOR A FEAST IS A LITTLE ATTENTION HERE AND THERE AND A SMALL AMOUNT OF YEAST."

"That is quite interesting," continued Jonathan. "I guess we will have to talk to the baker today."

"Besides I need some bread anyway," said Heather.

"We all have to find out what this means," said Michael. "I will need to start thinking seriously about what is in this book."

"So, what is yeast Heather?" asked Jonathan.

"I am not sure," she replied, "but I am sure we will need to talk to the baker. His bread is much different than mine."

"Yes," said Jonathan. "I noticed that the baker has special types of breads that are different than what I have seen and eaten throughout the country. Most of the bakers have a special secret. Maybe this is one of the magic potions that we must know about."

The three of them laughed nervously. They were not sure if there was magic or not even after all they had learned from the book.

Michael and Jonathan prepared the horse to go into town. As they were ready to leave, they noticed Heather selling more elixir to the young girl Teresa that sold bread around town.

Jonathan stopped her and asked, "How are things going?"

"Great," she replied. "I sell all the bottles of your potion that I can carry. It is an excellent product, and I am developing a large customer base."

"Excuse me," said Jonathan. "Would you have any idea what yeast is?"

"No," she explained, "but I do know it is something the baker puts into the bread to make it fat."

"Ah," said Jonathan. "So, the yeast is something special."

The boys said thank you and rode off into town.

"Well Michael," said Jonathan. "I think we better find a couple lads today and hire them to help us prepare more Vegetable Fair since the fair will start soon and we will need plenty of product available in order to meet the demand. If we do not have the product stocked and people start to ask for it and we cannot deliver, we could lose our business very fast."

"Yes," said Michael. "That is true. Customers become impatient fast. We must prepare for Christopher's stand, Heather's beverage stand, my stand, Teresa and many others that will want to take it with them. Judging by what Teresa is selling she will probably sell more than all of us."

"Yes," laughed Jonathan. "She is an ambitious lady always on the go. Possibly we should raise the price a little to slow down the demand. Besides the Baron claimed the drink was worth more than our present price. We will need to watch the price and volume closely to make sure we keep a reasonable profit without excessive work."

On the way into town, they passed the mill and Jeffrey waved to them.

"How are you doing Jeffrey?" asked Michael.

"Fine," he replied. "I talked to Steven this morning and he is interested in running your old beverage stand."

"Good," said Michael. "If he would like he can come with us now. We will take him into town and drop him at the stand. He can start working now while I continue to help Jonathan."

"He would like that," replied Jeffrey as he called out to Steven. "So, things are really going good huh?"

"Yes, the business is expanding rapidly," replied Michael.

"I don't understand it," said Jeffrey in a mumbled voice. "Nothing like that ever happens to me. I have thought about it for years and," Jeffrey pauses, "I don't know. I never get any opportunities."

Michael and Jonathan Looked at each other and could not believe their ears. Jeffrey was given the same opportunity and read the same book that they had read.

Shortly Steven came around the corner of the Mill and threw his bag into the back of the cart. The three boys headed into town and waved goodbye to Jeffrey.

When they approached the beverage stand, Michael jumped out and said, "Give me a few minutes to show Steven what needs to be done. I need to show him where things are. Then I can inform the owner a little later that I have other help here while I am moving on."

"Sure," replied Jonathan as he pulled the cart to the side of the road and watched the other travelers. Jonathan daydreamed a little while then started to think. The beverage stand business was going really well, the product was at all the stands, and he needed to make plans to expand out of the area. A lot of work will be required.

At the same time this business will not necessarily last all year and he must save some money to make it through the winter. Winters are long and cold here. Besides there must be something else that can be done. Surely there must be something he could do in the winter that other people will need or want.

The stable gets slow in the winter, but people still come and go. He really did not like the idea of going back to work at the stable, but he would if necessary. Business was great but he needed to give serious thought about future survival.

Michael returned and jumped in the cart saying, "Hey! Wake up Jonathan."

Jonathan came to his senses, looked over at Michael and said, "Yeah, I have been thinking. There is a lot in my mind."

"Let's go. We need to get to town and get things going. The day is passing quickly, and we need to get set up," said Michael. "My place is not much but I know I can make it nice enough to trap the business on my side of town. There is a lot of traffic by there, especially now that the fair is starting."

"Okay," said Jonathan. "Grab your things and we will get going."

The boys headed into town and as they passed thought the gate several people smiled acknowledging they were doing well.

Mr. Applebee said, "I see you have borrowed a cart from the Baron."

"No sir," replied Jonathan, proudly. "I rented the horse and cart. The Baron was kind enough to let me use them."

Mr. Applebee smiled and replied, "Nobody minds helping people that put out the ambition to succeed. You will find that more people are willing to help than you may expect."

Jonathan was excited about all the things going on. The fair had already started to bustle even though it was a week early.

Jonathan stopped the cart in front of the bake shop and said to Michael, "I need to find the solution to this riddle, and I am sure the baker holds some answers."

When the boys walked into the shop, they found the baker extremely busy. The baker needed to get up very early in the morning to get his work done. People stopped to buy from him before the sun came up. What a great business to know that your product will be sold before the day has hardly begun.

The baker greeted them warmly, "How are you young men today?"

"Fine sir," replied the boys.

He smiled at the young men and asked if they would like to have some bread.

Jonathan and Michael returned the smile and said, "Yes sir, you always have the most delicious bread."

The old man reached behind the counter and pulled out a couple of buns and handed them to the boys, stating, "These are something special I just baked. I made myself a little pan just for these."

"They are quite interesting," said Jonathan. "Look at that, they are all fluffy and filled out. This must have something to do with the riddle, I am sure."

"What riddle?" asked the baker.

"Let me read it to you," said Jonathan. "I need to know what yeast is?" Jonathan opened the book, turned to the correct page, and read the riddle once again.

"It is true the yeast does make the difference with the bread," replied the baker. "I believe what it says is that if you put yeast in the bread, the yeast will create air pockets and make the bread grow. If you are going to have a feast with a lot of people and do not use yeast, the bread will be thin and flat and does not look like much. But if you add a little yeast the bread will grow, and you can feed many people with the same amount of flower and other ingredients."

"So that is why," said Jonathan, "the book said the difference between the top and the bottom is something special, in this case it is yeast, and you can feed more."

"But tell me, **continued Jonathan. "what is yeast?"**

"That son is an old baker's secret. It is some kind of little animal that you cannot even see or at least, so I have been told. It only takes a small amount in the bread and the yeast is easy to produce. It grows like a mold on cheese," **answered the baker.**

Jonathan was amazed and asked, "Why doesn't everyone bake like this?"

"It is a baker's secret to keep us in business," **laughed the baker.** "And it does take some care to keep the yeast."

"Well sir," **said Michael.** "You always did make good bread, and everyone likes it. I am looking forward to eating your bread for a long time coming."

"I hate to disappoint you Michael," **said the baker.** "I am retiring at the end of the fair and returning home. You will need to find another baker."

"Who might that be?" asked Jonathan.

"I do not know," **replied the baker.** "It could be any or a number of people. I am sure someone will come in here and set up shop. There are a lot of bakers in the world."

"I should ask Heather," said Jonathan. "She is a very good cook, and she might know someone that wants to do some baking. Since you are leaving, maybe you can show me the secret of the yeast?"

"Sure Jonathan," answered the baker. "I really have no more secrets. Come on back and I will show you how to make the rolls."

Jonathan was excited and Michael did not want to get involved in making bread so he asked Jonathan if he could borrow the cart to continue setting up his business. Jonathan told Michael to pick up the barrels from Mr. Applebee, pick up the necessary bottles and get everything ready for his beverage stand. He could pick up the remaining materials and return to get Jonathan.

Jonathan spent more than an hour learning the baker's secrets. Fortunately, he had many written recipes that anyone that could read would be able to reproduce. Jonathan was especially interested in the small pan the baker had made to create the oven rolls. Jonathan was impressed about how the rolls were such a neat package. They had their own crusts so they would not dry out. They were like a miniature loaf of bread.

Jonathan thought this was a great idea and the wrong time for the baker to retire. The baker said he had done a lot in his life, and it was now time to rest. Jonathan thanked the baker, gathered the recipes the baker had given him and placed the special recipe for the rolls into his pocket. The baker also gave him the pan for the rolls.

Jonathan thanked the baker again and stepped into the street, watched the excitement of the people planning for the fair and decided he would have the blacksmith make him some pans to make rolls.

Michael was just returning from his chores. Jonathan jumped into the cart, and they headed out of town. They met Christopher at the gate as they were departing, and he already had a barrel in his cart when he addressed Jonathan.

"Hi Jonathan, I was just headed over to your place to pick up some more Vegetable Fair."

Jonathan knew it was time to return to help Heather and meeting Christopher saved him a trip to Christopher's house. "Come on over," said Jonathan. "We will mix a batch as soon as possible." Jonathan and Michael headed towards Heather's house with Christopher following.

On the way back to Heather's house they stopped by the fairground to watch a horse race. Christopher, Michael, and Jonathan talked as they watched the race. A young horse bolted out of the gate, down the track, around the tree and back to the finish line just ahead of the rest of the horses.

Christopher mentioned that he had seen this horse run many times and he always placed or beat the other horses by a nose. He is never far ahead, just a little bit better than the majority. He seems to have a special way of getting around the tree faster than other horses.

Jonathan thought about Christopher's words and said, "Yes isn't it interesting that those that are the best are really only a little better than average. That little bit seems to make all the difference between a nobody horse and a superstar." The men jumped back in their carts and headed down the road.

When they got back, the beverage stand was very busy. All four stumps were filled, several customers were in line and others were talking on the trail. Jonathan knew he had to get busy fast and get things ready for Heather. With Christopher there he would be extra busy mixing additional product. Jonathan jumped from the cart and unloaded the barrels and other products as fast as possible along with Michael. Jonathan helped Heather for a short period of time to shorten the line of customers.

Jonathan noticed Teresa standing on the trail selling bottles to waiting customers. Instantly he had an idea and he called her over.

She approached Jonathan, smiled, and asked, "Yes, can I help you?"

"Remember?" said Jonathan. "You said you would rather work with me than walk all over town. Let me give you the opportunity. Why don't you help Heather, and I will give you a percentage of all that you sell at the beverage stand? You will not need to walk the streets selling products unless you wish to. We will give you a job here at the stand working as a partner."

Heather liked the idea. She smiled and said, "That is what I need, help, because there are too many people for me to handle all at once. Besides we are doing much better business than I had expected."

With Teresa working it would free Heather to control the mixing of ingredients in order to keep their formula a secret. Heather and Jonathan started to mix a barrel of Vegetable Fair for Christopher to take back across town. They placed most of the raw ingredients into the barrel and then gave the barrel to Christopher's hired hand to start mixing.

Jonathan knew there would be a lot of people trying to duplicate the Vegetable Fair but after seeing some of the things Heather put into it and the detail of measurement, he knew they would be fairly safe for quite a while. The ingredients were simple, but it was true that if you did not put the correct amounts, you could easily spoil the drink. Also mixing large portions was harder than individual drinks as they had found on some first attempts. Jonathan then prepared another set of materials, mashed them into the barrel, and asked Michael to finish mixing while he took an inventory of materials for the next couple of days. Michael was glad to help, and he started to mix the potion almost immediately.

Jonathan told Teresa that he was going to take Heather with him to the Jenken's farm to try to get some more materials. Heather was elated because she had been stuck at her house for almost four days now and had not visited anybody except the people coming to her. This would give her an opportunity to go someplace and see what was going on. The two of them got into the cart and rode over to the Jenkens.

When they arrived, Mrs. Jenkens smiled and waved heartily, "I thought you would be coming back. I thought you would have been here a day ago. I have seen so much going on that I knew you would be by soon."

Jonathan smiled back and helped Heather down from the cart. Heather was a shrewd bargainer and Jonathan found that after a short period of time she had received a very good deal for the products needed. She had also secured an agreement for the products needed for a long period of time. She turned out to be quite a business partner.

Jonathan was happy about the relationship and stood quietly by as Heather reached into the cart for a couple bottles of Vegetable Fair and handed them to Mrs. Jenkens. "Here are a couple bottles I made special for you," said Heather.

Mrs. Jenkens was very excited and said, "I love this, and my children love it too. If you ever need anything Heather, please ask and we will provide whatever assistance we can."

It took Jonathan the better part of an hour to load the cart with all the vegetables that he needed. He started to think about all the volume expected and he knew he would need additional help. He was going to need to go to town today and hire several people. They could mix and distribute the product. Heather and he could prepare the formula and tend to other business.

Heather was very sneaky how she poured in the wine thought Jonathan as he laughed to himself. As soon as they arrived back at Heather's, Jonathan and Michael unloaded the wagon into the shed. The product took up most of the space in the shed leaving just enough room for Jonathan to sleep. Jonathan did not mind because the crowded space represented success.

Heather apologized when she saw the small room and realized Jonathan had little space to sleep.

Jonathan said, "Do not worry I am comfortable and happy where I am, but I do have something else in mind. Would you like to take another ride Heather since Teresa is doing very well at the stand? All the barrels are full except the one Michael is mixing to take to his place."

Heather nodded yes and the three climbed into the cart and headed toward the old mill.

They stopped and overlooked the large field. "See the old cottage down by the stream?" asked Jonathan.

"Yes," replied Heather. "I remember this place. I have been here many times to watch people fish in the stream."

"I want to get this place," said Jonathan with confidence. "I want to use it for our business. We will have lots of storage and it will be perfect for additional business when the fair is over."

"What!" said Heather. "We haven't finished what we started, yet you are looking ahead."

"I am not losing my focus," comforted Jonathan. "I am only planning for the extra growth and storage. We need to be close to the water since the major ingredient is water. We waste a lot of time and effort carrying water. We can make much more product close to the stream and I can make a small mill to mix the ingredients using the power of the water. I also have some other ideas that I have been meaning to talk to you about. Here, try some of this."

He pulled out some of the rolls he had gotten from the baker and handed one to Heather. "Heather, look at the rolls." They looked like a loaf of bread but only a couple inches in diameter.

"I have never seen anything quite like this before," said Heather.

"The baker made a special pan to cook these," said Jonathan as he pulled the pan from his pack. "I also have the recipe," continued Jonathan as he reached for the small paper in his pocket. "I also found out what yeast is."

Heather was surprised, "You did all that this morning even with everything else that is going on?"

"Yes," said Jonathan. "I really believe this is something we can do. Your vegetables are good for the summer, and we can store lots of the material for the winter. We can place the mixture in bottles and store them in the stream to keep them cold once we have control of the pond. During winter we could move them into storage. This way we should be able to sell your Vegetable Fair most of the year. We will not be able to purchase new ingredients or produce product late in the year. Also, I was thinking about the bread. We could make the bread here and specialize in the rolls. Did you know the baker was retiring?"

Heather shook her head no.

Johnathan continued, "I was thinking we could manufacture the yeast, bottle it, store it and provide yeast so that people could raise their bread just like the baker."

Heather thought quietly and said, "I must consider this. These ideas are all new and they are not yet in my mind. I like the idea of a larger area for more storage. This is a big dream Jonathan, and it will take a lot of work."

Jonathan knew it would take a lot of work, but he did not mind.

They stopped the cart, got out and walked around to look at the old cottage. The cottage was fair enough. It had a nice inside living room built around a huge fireplace. There was a dining area separated on one side, a bedroom on the other side and a quest room to the back. Jonathan thought this was quite a cottage and much finer than most in the area, which only had one room. What more could a person ask for? Jonathan was excited about the idea.

Heather asked, "How could you afford such a cottage? We cannot spend all our savings on this and besides the Baron still uses this as a vacation home. You don't even know if he would be willing to sell the place."

"Well," said Jonathan. "I am going to find out. I will ask the Baron at my next opportunity and see if he will let me use the cottage. Possibly I can make a business arrangement or partnership with him."

Heather smiled at Jonathan. She knew Jonathan felt true in his heart about his plan.

The two of them headed back toward Heather's house. "I will need to return the cart as soon as I have delivered the barrel to Michael's beverage stand," said Jonathan. "I will return later this evening."

"Fine," replied Heather. "Maybe we can look at the book and solve another riddle. We can gather the people together and make some plans for the next day."

Heather hurried out of the wagon because Teresa was overwhelmed by customers. There were many more than when Heather was working. Wondering why, Jonathan approached Teresa to discover her success.

Teresa stated, "From my part of my profit I decided to provide small samples. I placed small samples on the counter for customers walking by. If they like the product, they purchase a bottle to take with them or they try some at the stand."

"What a great idea!" said Heather. "Little things make a big difference. Forget about taking the samples out of your profit since the idea more than pays for itself."

The samples were too small to quench the traveler's thirst, yet it was almost guaranteed to capture a sale.

Michael and Jonathan loaded a barrel of Vegetable Fair into the cart and headed for Michael's beverage stand. They secured the barrel in Michael's cottage. Jonathan requested Michael to join them for the evening, grab Jeffrey on the way and try to solve another riddle.

Michael said he would be delighted and would come over after preparing things for his first day of business tomorrow.

Jonathan returned to the stable knowing he would need the cart again soon in another day or two and he did not want the stable master upset. As Jonathan approached the stable, he noticed the Baron watering his horse at the trough. Jonathan approached the Baron after tying up the horse. "Excuse me sir," said Jonathan.

"Why sure young Jonathan," said the Baron in a cheerful voice. "I always enjoy talking to you. What is in your mind?"

"Well sir," started Jonathan. "I am going to need the horse and cart for more than just one day. It will be very expensive at a daily rate, and I was wondering if I could get a longer rate such as monthly?"

"That sounds like an idea Jonathan, a monthly rental is not something I thought about before. You could use the horse a certain amount of time and bring it back daily. I have a steady customer and you get a reduced rate. I like the idea," said the Baron.

"Someday soon," said Jonathan, "I will need to buy a horse and cart from your stable."

"Oh, so business is going that good?" questioned the Baron.

"Yes sir," said Jonathan. "Things really are going that good."

The Baron noted that Jonathan wanted to say something, but he was too reserved to start the conversation. "Go ahead lad. What do you want to say?" asked the Baron. "There must be something more on your mind."

"Yes sir, there is," started Jonathan. "I have been noticing the old cottage at the mill by the pond that you lived in when you started the mill."

"Yes son?" injected the Baron.

"Well," continued Jonathan. "I have been wondering how much the rent would be on a place like that because I have been thinking about expanding my business and I need a much larger place."

"That is an awful bold step Jonathan, to start out like this," **said the Baron.** "That cottage is much larger and more expensive than most in the town. You want to start your business with a huge overhead and the business may only last a few weeks."

"No sir, I have a much larger plan," **continued Jonathan confidently.** "I am sure the vegetable business will last long beyond the fair. We are already expanding the customer base. I have Christopher across town, Michael on one side, Heather on the other side and only one entrance is not covered yet. I feel we can build enough customers and by using the bottles for storage and keeping them cool enough in the pond, we should be able to maintain the business long into and possibly through the winter."

"That is definitely an ambitious plan young man, and it will require a lot of work on your part." **said the Baron.**

"Yes sir," **replied Jonathan.** "I know it will take effort, but a lot of the farmers have a problem in winter with a continuing income. The farmers could extend credit to me by selling their vegetables now and I could make payments in the winter when they need the money. I should have enough profit to make payments to you for the cottage. Also, at the same time I have additional plans."

The Baron's eyebrows rose, he observed Jonathan intently and asked, "Other plans son? Are you losing track of your goals already?"

"Oh no sir," replied Jonathan quickly. "This is all part of my plan, and it all works together. The mill is right next door and I thought that during the winter months when vegetables are not growing, that I might be able to get flour from the mill and bake some bread for sale."

"Yes Jonathan, but we have a baker," said the Baron.

"Yes sir," replied Jonathan. "But the baker is leaving town and I want to specialize in these rolls. Here try one of these sir." Jonathan handed a roll to the Baron.

The Baron looked at the roll and tasted it. "Yes," he said, "These are very good, and they are practical. They are the right size for a traveler to carry."

"I have the recipe," said Jonathan. "The secret of the roll has to do with yeast. I should be able to produce the bread all winter. With the Vegetable Fair and bread and a little meat a person could survive quite well."

The Baron studied Jonathan acutely, watching every move and listening to every word Jonathan said.

"Not only what I have said but the cottage could be used as an inn. It is a lot larger than what I need for sleeping. I do not intend to use the cottage for travelers to sleep, but only for a place to stop for bread, Vegetable Fair and a few small food items. There is plenty of room in the dining and living area to entertain many customers. I could partition the cottage to provide privacy and still accommodate many customers. The cottage would provide a small area to socialize while waiting to take bread and Vegetable Fair home with them."

"Sounds like something I have seen in other lands that they call a restaurant," said the Baron. "The difference would be that you only offer a limit menu more like a tavern."

"Yes sir," said Jonathan. "We may be able to offer more once we are established and can afford to hire some help. I know it takes a lot of work and I only have Heather to help me at the present."

The Baron smiled, "I am happy you are still working with Heather. She is a good woman, and you make a very good team."

"Yes sir, she is a good partner," said Jonathan.

"I would not mind having you as my partner also Jonathan," said the Baron. "And by the way son you can use the cottage. I will take the rent as you can produce it and we will work out the percentage as part of a business agreement. You can start by moving your belongings over as soon as you like."

Jonathan thanked the Baron with demonstrated excitement.

Jonathan grabbed his pack and headed back to tell Heather. He did not stop and ran all the way back to the cottage. "Heather!" said Jonathan excitedly. "I have a new place to sleep tonight if I want."

"Oh," said Heather. "Where are you going?"

"Do you remember the cottage?" continued Jonathan. "The Baron has decided to be partners with us. He is going to loan us the cottage for a percentage and let us start with the plan I have in mind."

Heather showed some sign of distress and Jonathan noted it in her eyes.

"Don't worry Heather," said Jonathan in a soothing voice. "I will be helping you and we will be close. Besides you are a big part of my plans and I need you."

Heather smiled shyly and turned back to her work.

Jonathan reminded Heather that Jeffrey and Michael were coming over that evening for a little social activity. He also wanted to share the answer to the last riddle and see if they could provide help for the next one.

It had been a busy day and by the time the four of them had gathered together for the evening they were all quite tired.

"I found the answer to the last riddle," stated Jonathan.

They all motioned Jonathan to continue.

"The samples Teresa gave to the customers, the horse that wins by his special ability to get around the tree, the special rolls the baker makes are all examples of a little extra detail. The little bit of effort sets them apart from everyone else, nothing big or major, just something small and special lets them excel over all their competition."

All three nodded with acknowledgment that Jonathan had found the answer to the riddle.

Chapter 16
View

"Okay," said Jeffrey. "What is the next fantasy in your book?"

Jonathan excused himself and retrieved the book from his pack in the shed. As he returned to the table and opened the book Heather made a comment, "What is all this writing you have in the book?"

"Oh," said Jonathan. "I have been writing notes down in the margin of the book to help remind me what each riddle means. This could be important to me in the future."

"That is a good idea," said Heather.

"What a bunch of gobbledygook," said Jeffrey. "You don't even know if any of this is real or even if you are writing down the right thing or not. How do you know if what you are writing down is correct?"

"I don't," said Jonathan. "But it really doesn't matter as long as it brings me success."

Jonathan turned the pages to the next riddle and read the words,

"A CANDLELIGHT SHINING IN A MIRROR LOOKS QUITE DIFFERENT IF YOU ARE FAR OR NEAR."

"If you ask me," said Jeffrey, "you are all wasting your time with a bunch of trivia."

"Ah don't be a spoiled sport," **said Heather. "Let's have some fun. I will get some candles out and a mirror and we can do like last time."**

"It sounds like the same riddle as last time if you ask me," **said Jeffrey. "Just like the last time we used a candle."**

"No, I don't think so," **said Heather. "There is always something different we need to learn."**

Jonathan took the candle and mirror from Heather and placed them by the shed so that it would reflect the light back to where they were sitting.

"This is ridiculous," **said Jeffrey.** "Anyway, my eyes are really good, and I can see the candle and its reflection in the mirror. That is what I see. What do you see Michael?"

"Let me be the one close up," **said Michael.** "Jeffrey is the one far away."

Michael got up from the bench, walked over to the candle and knelt down by the mirror.

"What do you see?" **asked Heather.**

"It is kind of neat," **replied Michael.** "I see the candle, I see my face, I see the clothes I am wearing. I can see the outline of the courtyard where you are sitting. I can see some of the grass, trees and leaves. It is quite a different view from where I am at and where Jeffrey is sitting."

"The last time, with the unlit candle, we all saw something different with the same view," said Heather. "This time we all have a different view of the same thing. Now we need to find out how that pertains to success."

"It is about time for me to go to bed," said Jeffrey. "I need to be leaving. I think you have all let this magic stuff go to your head. Good night, I will see you tomorrow."

"Good night, Jeffrey," replied Jonathan.

Michael also got up to return to his place. Jonathan said good night to Heather and went to the shed after walking Heather to the house.

That morning at breakfast Jonathan informed Heather that she was completely correct about her solution to the riddle.

"Heather," said Jonathan. "It is true that Jeffrey has no view of success. His view of success is that there is no such thing or success is only for others. My view of success is just now growing and is not fully defined as to what I want in life. The Baron's view of success is an empire, and the stable master's view of success is power. Each one of us has a different idea about the same thing. We are all looking at success, but success is different for different people. I cannot expect to force what I want onto other people and likewise I would not let them force unto me what they think success is to them."

"It did not take you long to solve that riddle," said Heather. "You are now finding answers in your sleep."

Jonathan laughed and said, "Not completely in my sleep. Besides you had the answer, I only tied it to my life." Jonathan opened his book to write down the new meaning of the parable.

Mrs. Becket noticed that Jonathan was looking through the book and asked Jonathan, "What is the next chapter in the magic story?"

Chapter 17
Risk
Summary Three

Jonathan turned the page and read the following out loud,

"AN EAGLE WOULD LACK WINGS, HAVE FINS MADE OUT OF SCALE, IF IT DID NOT TAKE THE PLUNGE AND LEARN HOW TO SAIL."

"I guess is says an eagle would not be such a grand bird but might as well be a fish if it did not try to fly," **said Jonathan.** "The Storyteller told me one time that the eagle builds a nest high on a mountain cliff. When the baby bird is ready to leave the nest, he is coaxed or pushed out by the mother. Can you imagine the fear of falling or jumping from a cliff even before you know you can fly? I guess it is another sign of bravery for a powerful, majestic bird."

"I do not believe it has anything to do with bravery," **said Mrs. Becket.** "Not only will I give you breakfast today but I also have the answer to your riddle."

Jonathan and Heather looked at her in surprise. "You know the answer already?" **questioned Heather.**

"The answer is simple my child," **continued Mrs. Becket.** "It is a good chance the eagle will fly when the mother pushes the young from the nest. As for you and Jonathan, you have a good chance of doing successful business at the mill cottage. Like the eagle that must try his wings, Jonathan has dared to talk to the Baron, quit his job in light of possible bad consequences, and invested everything to try to get his business going. Very few people undertake such bold challenges and consequently there are only a few as grand as eagles in the world."

Heather asked, "So tell me Jonathan, what have you learned these past few days?"

Jonathan sat silently pondering Mrs. Becket's words before answering. "I have learned that there are many ways to accomplish a task. My way may or may not be the best, but I must keep my eyes and ears open and be prepared to accept other people's ideas as well as my own. I learned I must season my dreams with the power of expectation. Dreams must be truly believed and come from the heart to come true. I must be specific about what I desire because what I truly desire, I will receive. I found that all great things in life and the most successful are only a little better than average. I must find something special in life and master it to my benefit. I learned that success means something different to everyone. What appears to be a success to me could appear as a failure to you. Only I can visualize my own success since only I know and understand my own goals. Finally, I must be willing to take a reasonable risk if I ever expect great success."

"That is excellent," replied Mrs. Becket. "Surely you are obtaining the knowledge of a magic far more useful than the fantasy of witches. Now what does the next parable have to say?"

Chapter 18
Help

Jonathan opened the book and read the next few lines,

"EVERYONE NEEDS YOU BUT WATCH OUT THE PAIN. A SMALL GROUP WILL WANT YOU AND REMEMBER YOUR NAME."

"That is a strange one," **said Heather.** "How could someone that needs you hurt you? I do not understand. I needed my father when he was alive, and I never hurt him."

"I don't fully understand it," **said Jonathan, "but I do know Jeffrey needs me and I think I will drop off a couple bottles so he can make a little extra money."**

"That would be a good idea," **said Heather.** "He needs a little boost to start thinking about success."

Jonathan and Heather smiled at each other. Jonathan grabbed several bottles as he went out the door and headed into town. Jonathan shouted good morning to Jeffrey across the small field.

"Good morning, Jonathan," **replied Jeffrey.** "What are you up to so early in the morning?"

"Well," **said Jonathan.** "I thought I would get out and do some public relations work, see how things are going and try to get an idea of how much product I need. By the way I have a couple bottles I would like to give them to you as a gift. You can sell them and make a few extra pennies for something you might like."

"No," said Jeffrey. "I really don't have the time for that. By the way I will wake up Steven and he can go with you to the beverage stand."

Jonathan was a little hurt from the unexpected reply from Jeffrey. "I will wait," said Jonathan.

Steven appeared almost immediately, they headed into town and on the way, they encountered Teresa.

"Morning Jonathan," said Teresa. "I am going to get an extra head start at the beverage stand. We made a very good profit yesterday. You know I live on the other side of town, and you don't have a beverage stand there yet and I am thinking seriously about opening over there if you don't mind."

"That sounds like a great idea," said Jonathan. "But I will need to find someone to replace you since Heather needs help at her place."

"Sure," said Teresa. "Take whatever time is necessary. I will see you later."

As Jonathan and Steven approached the beverage stand, they noticed Michael talking to the owner. As they got closer it was obvious that Michael had just completed the sale of a couple bottles of product to the owner.

"He is not wasting any time," said Jonathan. "He has sold product to one of the customers I had intended to talk to this morning. No problem though because it is all part of the business. Good morning, Michael," continued Jonathan to Michael.

"Good morning, Jonathan," replied Michael. "How are things going with you today? You are up real early."

"Yeah, I am just out taking a look around to get an idea about how the business is doing and trying to find out what I need to satisfy the customers. There are a lot of new people in town," said Jonathan.

"That is for sure," replied Michael.

"By the way Michael," said Jonathan as he handed two bottles to Michael. "Why don't you take these as a token for what you have done for me?"

"Gee thanks," said Michael. "I really appreciate this. I haven't even made much profit for you, and you are already giving things away."

"That's what friends are for," said Jonathan. "I knew you would appreciate it and do something good with it."

"You bet I will Jonathan," said Michael. "I will also put in extra time today that will probably make you more profit than the cost of your gift."

Jonathan bid good-bye to everyone and headed back toward the stable. He wanted to get there soon knowing the Baron would be there early and he did not want to be late. He wanted to make sure he had closed the business deal.

As Jonathan approached the stable, he saw the stable master working in the yard. "Good morning, how are you doing?" asked Jonathan.

"Oh, I am doing okay, how about yourself?" asked the stable master."

"I am doing really good," replied Jonathan. "In fact, I have been doing excellently. I thought you might want to sell a couple bottles at the stable for some extra income. There are a lot of people that come to the stable especially during the fair. It would be an ideal place to catch travelers."

"Not me!" snapped the stable master. "I don't want anything to do with that brew. Besides you will be back shortly. It will pass."

"Well, even if it passes," said Jonathan. "You might make quite a few pennies on the side. Anyway, what can it hurt?"

"I don't need your help Jonathan," chided the stable master. "I don't need anything from you."

Jonathan stopped and reflected for a few minutes. "That is not true," said Jonathan.

"It is not that you don't need me, it is that you don't want my help."

Jonathan walked away politely and met the Baron coming in the gate. Jonathan completed his business quickly with the Baron and ran back to the beverage stand as fast as he could go.

"Heather! Heather!" he shouted. "We have to get our things ready and take them down to the cottage. We get to move in today. By the way, I found the answer to the riddle. Strange as it may seem it does make sense."

"Oh," said Heather. "And what is it?"

"It is quite simple," began Jonathan. "Everyone needs everyone else's help. I need your help; you need mine. We all need each other, and we believe other people need us, so we try hard to help them. I tried to help Jeffrey make extra income because I know he needs it. I tried to help the stable master to make extra income because I felt he needed it. They both need the income but neither Jeffrey nor the stable master wanted my help and that is the secret. Michael on the other hand wants my help and likewise so does Teresa. We must spend our time with the people that want our help and not waste our time trying to help those that need our help that do not want our help. They can still be our friends, but we must not waste our time and energy trying to do something they do not want us to do."

Chapter 19
Empathy

Jonathan and Heather informed Mrs. Becket that they were going to move their belongings over to the old millhouse and start business there.

Mrs. Becket replied that someone would need to stay and run the beverage stand and she had already made plans with Mrs. Jenkens to work as partners keeping the stand open. This arrangement was perfect since Teresa was going to move to her stand on the other side of town.

Jonathan was happy that things were working out so well. At that moment Christopher rode up with his cart to pick up a barrel he needed for his stand.

"Morning Christopher," said Jonathan.

Christopher replied back, "Morning Jonathan, how is business?"

"I am doing fine," replied Jonathan. "You got here at the right time Christopher. I need a horse and cart today and I am wondering if I could borrow one from you?"

"That is a good idea Jonathan," continued Christopher. "In fact, I do not have the money on me right now to pay for the barrel. Maybe we can do an exchange of products? You use the cart and extend me some credit on an extra barrel of product if you want. We can both make something from the deal."

"That is an excellent idea," said Jonathan. "In fact, maybe we can work out a long-term arrangement. I may need several horses and carts especially during the fair and I may need your services as well as the Baron's."

Jonathan went into the shed and started to pack his belongings for moving to the old mill cottage. While he was packing, he opened the book, wrote down a few notes on what he had just found out and read the next chapter,

"ASHES TO ASHES AND DUST TO DUST, EACH PART OF THE UNIVERSE IS MADE OUT OF US."

Jonathan was a little perplexed. He wanted an immediate answer to his riddles because his business was moving so fast that he wanted success now and did not want to wait. He felt this riddle may take extra effort to solve but he planned to solve it no matter what.

Heather's bright smile as he exited the shed immediately overcame Jonathan's minor depression. He laughed with her as they walked to the cart to check things out.

Jonathan rapidly loaded the cart with belongings and product. Christopher was a hard worker and he found that he loaded the cart much faster than expected. He had to work harder than normal to keep up with Christopher.

Heather, Jonathan, and Christopher climbed into the cart and headed to the mill. As they passed the mill heading to the cottage, Jeffrey came out and greeted them a good morning.

"Good morning, Jeffrey, how are you?" said Jonathan.

"Oh, I don't know," replied Jeffrey. "I have been feeling pretty sick lately. I think the flu has come over me. I have had a headache, feeling tired and rundown. I talked to Michael about it, and he said he felt a little bad too. How about you guys? Have you caught the flu?"

Heather's smile faded slightly, and she said, "Yes, you know I noticed lately that I have not been feeling the best since I got up now that you mentioned it."

Jonathan looked at Jeffrey and Heather, shrugged his shoulders and said, "Nope, not me. I am feeling fine."

They continued on to the old cottage. Jonathan looked at Heather and asked, "Are you really feeling bad?"

Heather waited a few moments before answering, "I really don't know. I thought I was feeling bad."

"Well," said Jonathan, "I am not having any problems. I am feeling fine. I don't think it is any kind of flu or anything we may have eaten."

Heather sat for a few minutes and her smile started to return. "I guess I am fine," she stated. "I guess it was just thinking about it or maybe I was a little tired."

When the three of them reached the mill house, they noticed the Baron was there with a couple of people. Everyone was fixing and cleaning the cottage and area. The Baron was singing and whistling off in the distance.

Jonathan approached the Baron, "Good morning, sir, how are you today?"

"I am doing great!" replied the Baron. "I have not had this much fun in a long time. I always feel good when a bit of excitement is around."

Heather and Jonathan helped and before long everyone was happy and bubbly. They got back into the cart and headed back for another load of belongings.

"I have an answer to the new riddle already," said Jonathan.

"What riddle?" asked Christopher.

Jonathan showed the riddle to Christopher and Heather and then explained, "I was a little depressed this morning when I did not understand the riddle, but your smile cheered me immediately Heather. Later on, when Jeffrey said he was sick, his sickness made Heather feel bad. Later on, you were not sure of your condition when I said I was not sure about the flu. Finally, when we came across the Baron, his cheery attitude changed our attitudes completely. You see Heather; it is very simple because everybody affects everybody. The way we feel and the way we act affects the way others feel and the way others act. We must be careful that we don't get others depressed and likewise we must not let others depress us. We must try to make good cheer all of the time. Or as the riddle says, everyone is made of everyone else and everything and everyone effects everyone."

"I was once told that it is impossible to look up and force a big smile and still feel bad or mad," **said Christopher.**

"Next time someone gets me down, I will do just that, look up and smile," **said Heather.**

Chapter 20
Plan

"What is in your little book anyway?" asked Christopher.

"It is a manual of magic potions for success," replied Jonathan. "I will show you how it works."

Jonathan opened the book and read the next line,

"FOR THE WORM TIME IS LACKING, BUT THE WOODPECKER KEEPS ON WHACKING."

"That is strange," said Christopher. "What in the world could a worm and a woodpecker have to do with success?"

"They really don't," said Heather. "But they point the way to understanding. You know it has something to do with the worm being lazy or slow and the woodpecker keeping at it no matter how hard the wood is until he finally gets the worm."

You mean I need to be hardheaded?" laughed Christopher.

"No," said Heather. "I think Jeffrey is an example. He always complains he has no time to sell product, but he spends most of the day waiting for someone to bring grain to make flour."

"Yes," interrupted Jonathan. "The stable master spends hours daily complaining to travelers that he has no time to go fishing. If he would spend only part of the time fishing instead of talking, he would have more time fishing than he would ever want. I am guilty too. I carried a broken bucket for almost six months and complained about the lost water without taking the time to fix it. When I finally made up my mind to stop talking, it only took an hour to repair the bucket."

"I never see Christopher waste any time," said Heather. "Also, I am proud how you Jonathan are always spending your present time doing something useful."

"I guess the book has taught me some valuable habits," said Jonathan. "I will need to always have a book handy so when I have idle time, I can exercise my brain."

"The answer to your riddle appears to have been found," said Christopher. "Like the woodpecker, you must undertake big projects a bite at a time and do not be like the worm spending your time going nowhere. Every minute is important and what you do with your time determines your success."

Chapter 21
Attitude

Jonathan was pleased with the quick answer to his riddle and sang the rest of the way back to Heather's house. After returning Heather, they loaded the cart with Christopher's barrel. They decided to let Heather finish things at the house while Christopher took the barrel back to his place so that his hired hand could sell the product.

Jonathan decided to ride into town to try and get the blacksmith to make him some pans for rolls. On the way into town Jonathan opened the book and read the next chapter,

"SMILE WHEN THEY FROWN AND LAUGH WHEN THEY SMILE DRIVES YOU ON AN EXTRA MILE."

The blow of the bugle interrupted Jonathan's thoughts. People were moving everywhere as the King and his escorts departed town. It was obvious they were on their way for a day of hunting. Jonathan bowed respectfully and was surprised when the King tipped his hat and winked at him.

Jonathan had not fully gained his composure when he was addressed by the Duke. "Good afternoon young Jonathan. I would like you to bring a couple bottles of your elixir by my castle tomorrow and the

King requests you bring a bottle to him tomorrow at two o'clock."

"Ye ... yes sir," said Jonathan dumbfounded. He could not believe the King, or the Duke even knew who he was.

"It appears your success has made you famous," said Christopher. "I shall return in an hour to help you finish your move."

Jonathan thanked Christopher and walked into town still in a daze from his experience with the King.

"Good afternoon, sir," said Jonathan to the blacksmith.

"And a good day it tizz," replied the blacksmith. His shop was neat and clean in spite of the hot dirty work he performed all day long. He had a round face and a pudgy nose and beard as white as snow. He was known to be the happiest man in the valley. The blacksmith was known to be able to make anything and Jonathan suspected that he was Santa Clause preparing each day for Christmas.

The blacksmith reached into the hot fire with his tongs and pulled out a red-hot horseshoe. He dropped it into a bucket of water and the steam filled the room like an early morning fog. The blacksmith jumped with joy and exclaimed, "Another perfect shoe!"

He laid it on the table in front of Jonathan. Jonathan noticed the word Baron in raised letters on the shoe and was about to pick it up to examine it when the blacksmith called him, "Stop lad! Either it does not take you long to look at a horseshoe or you plan to burn your hand since that is still awful hot."

Jonathan smiled at the blacksmith's humor and thanked him for preventing a burn. "It must be hard to work over a hot fire all day," said Jonathan.

"Life is what you make it lad, and nothing is hard for me," replied the blacksmith. "The shoe is cool now if you want to look at it."

Jonathan inspected the shoe. "This is truly a work of art," said Jonathan.

"I always try to put a touch of beauty into my work," replied the blacksmith. "It gives me a sense of pride and accomplishment. So, what can I do for you today, Jonathan?"

"Well sir, I need some pans made like this one," said Jonathan.

"And what do you plan on doing with the pan?" asked the blacksmith.

Jonathan took a roll from his pack and handed it to the blacksmith. "I plan on making these for sale sir, try one," said Jonathan.

"This is very good," said the blacksmith. "So, you want to become a baker as well as a beverage stand owner."

"Not really sir," answered Jonathan. "I only intend to specialize in these rolls."

"That could be a shrewd decision Jonathan," stated the blacksmith. "I know a little about baking myself. How many rolls a day do you intend to make and how often will you bake?"

"I am not sure?" answered Jonathan with a question in his eyes. "Fifty to five hundred if business is good."

"You also need a good oven," said the blacksmith. "How about if I make you a small oven and pan combination that will produce fifty rolls an hour? That way you can control the amount of bread with low overhead and less effort."

"I like that idea," said Jonathan. "Since Heather will do most of the baking, I am sure she will like it even more than I. How many weeks before you will be done."

"How about today lad?" replied the blacksmith with a jolly laugh. "I am sure you would like to have it ready for the fair."

Jonathan was elated. He thanked the blacksmith and went outside to await the arrival of Christopher.

I know the meaning of the riddle, thought Jonathan. *My time passed rapidly when I was with the blacksmith. The work you do will remain the same so you might as well enjoy yourself the entire time. If you feel mad or bad about your work, you will*

only prolong the day. **Jonathan promised himself to always keep a positive outlook on life and his work.**

Jonathan reached the gate just as Christopher arrived. Jonathan greeted Christopher with a smile and jumped into the cart. "What a wonderful day," said Jonathan.

"You sure seem happy," said Christopher. "What is the occasion for your high spirit?"

Jonathan smiled, "The book just told me that every occasion is an occasion for high spirit."

In no time they had finished moving the remainder of their belongings to the mill cottage. Plans were made for a big party that evening to celebrate the beginning of what was sure to be a big success.

It was early evening and Christopher was the last to arrive. "Hey Jonathan," said Christopher. "The blacksmith asked me to deliver this to you. I don't know what it is, but he said you would know what to do with it. He sent a note on how to operate it."

Jonathan could not believe his eyes that the blacksmith could do such a good job in such a short time. He placed the oven next to the cottage kitchen door and told Heather about it.

Heather, Mrs. Jenkens and Heather's mother were preparing food for the evening and Michael and Jeffrey were gathering firewood. Even the stable master and the Baron had shown up for the party. It was definitely going to be a good evening, thought Jonathan.

After several hours of eating and talking Heather brought out a bunch of hot fresh rolls. Jonathan prepared a toast with Vegetable Fair, and everyone savored the taste of the rolls.

Chapter 22
Judgment

Jonathan opened the book, and everyone listened as he read,

"GRAND EMBELLISHMENTS OF CASTLE WALLS TO IMPRESS THE PASSER BY, OFTEN LEADS TO EMPTY HALLS AND THE OWNER ASKING WHY."

"What a timely saying," said Christopher. "Jonathan has been invited to two castles tomorrow, the Duke and the King."

The King!" exclaimed Heather.

"The Duke!" said the Baron with even greater surprise.

Everyone looked at the Baron with questions in their eyes. "Not even the King has been to the Duke's castle," continued the Baron. "He has the most beautiful castle in all the land. For that matter it is the most magnificent I have ever seen. Surely it is many times better than the King's castle. No one knows the guests he entertains or anything about him. He is a strange quiet man."

"Tomorrow I am sure I will find the secret and let you all know what I find," said Jonathan.

The party lasted until late evening, and everyone returned home knowing that the fair would bring them all more success this year than ever before in the past.

Jonathan woke up early, grabbed several bottles of Vegetable Fair and half a dozen rolls. It was several miles to the Duke's castle, and he knew it would take a couple hours to walk there. He also had to return in time for his appointment with the King. Jonathan enjoyed the walk, and he needed the rest from the hectic few days before.

The Duke's castle was at the edge of the ocean and Jonathan could hear the sound of the waves washing the shore. *What a beautiful view,* thought Jonathan as he approached the gate. *I believe anyone would want to live here.*

Jonathan noticed there were no guards at the gate as he entered the courtyard. The entire courtyard was made of marble. The beauty almost took Jonathan's breath away. The fountain was crystal clear and sparkled like diamonds in the sun.

Jonathan knocked on the internal door and waited a long time before the Duke arrived. Jonathan wondered where the servants were as the Duke closed the door behind them.

"Good morning, Jonathan," said the Duke with a bright smile. "Come this way and we shall have some breakfast."

Though the castle was magnificent their footsteps produced lonely echoes with every step. Jonathan could not restrain himself from asking, "Where are the people? Is it a holiday or are they all still asleep?"

"That is a long story," said the Duke as his smile turned to sorrow.

"Well," said Jonathan. "I have a good ear if you would like to share the story with me?"

Jonathan placed two bottles and the bread on the table.

"Thank you for bringing the drink Jonathan and what is this?" said the Duke pointing to the bread.

"Something special I brought as a gift," replied Jonathan.

"Delicious!" said the Duke. He continued saying, "I was not always a rich man. In fact, I was very poor. My father departed on the crusades when I was very young. My mother died of the plague, and I had no relatives that anyone knew. Since no one could contact my father, I was placed in an orphanage. I spent many years there sharing shoes and clothes with my many orphanage brothers and sisters. Often, we had but one meal a day. Though I was poor, strangely I was very happy. As the years passed, I grew into a young man working hard at any job but still wondering about my family. Then a few years ago a courier located me. He said he was looking for me for a long time. My father had died and left his estate to me should the courier be able to find me."

"Please continue," said Jonathan encouraging the Duke.

The Duke continued, "Of course as you can see the wealth was extensive. My father had made a fortune in his travels but was never able to locate my mother or myself. I wanted everything I never had including a high status, so I moved far from my land of birth and appeared here as the rich duke. I wanted everyone to notice me, so I built this wonderful castle; dressed fancy and pretended I was much better than everyone else. Unfortunately, I was never happy. My superior attitude made it difficult to obtain good help. I was always being questioned and soon I had no desire to have anyone around since no one appeared to be a true friend. When I heard of your rapid success, I knew I must speak to you to see if you could help."

There was a look of desperation in the Duke's eyes.

"I would love to help," **said Jonathan with a huge smile.** "As a matter of fact, I have a magic book of success and I read your portion only yesterday. Let us read the book together."

Jonathan opened the book and once again read the riddle to the Duke.

"You see," **said Jonathan.** "Just as your castle is beautiful outside and empty inside, you have placed a shell around yourself. You are living a dream trying to impress everyone when in reality you were a far better and happier person before. There is nothing wrong with great wealth, but it must not affect your vanity. Why don't you open your castle as a magnificent lodge? You could employ many peasants providing a needed source of income, yet you could entertain royalty and travelers from around the country and earn the respect and friendship of many. Remove the phony wall and place yourself equal to everyone."

"I shall start today!" said the Duke with a look of hope in his eyes. "I will have my grand opening at the start of the fair. Please Jonathan, pass the word that I will need many employees starting today."

Jonathan said he would inform people right away.

"What all does your book have to say?" asked the Duke.

"There is too much to tell today sir," answered Jonathan. "Maybe I can come back during your grand opening and discuss it further with you then. In the meantime, let us read the next chapter."

"I would like that," said the Duke.

Chapter 23
Sharing

Jonathan opened the book and read,

"WHERE DOES THE BROOK STOP AND THE OCEAN WATERS BEGIN? THERE IS NO LINE OF DISTINCTION THEY ARE TANGLED TIGHT WITHIN."

"You are at the right place to start solving the riddle," said the Duke. "The brook enters the ocean just north of my castle."

Jonathan placed the book back in his pack, thanked the Duke for his hospitality and headed back toward town.

On his way back Jonathan sat down by the brook and watched the stream flow into the ocean. Gentle wave after wave moved and swirled the water. The ocean water was salty, and the brook was fresh, but Jonathan could not find where one stopped and the other began. Soon he grabbed his pack and hurried to town so that he would not miss his meeting with the King.

When Jonathan arrived in town he waved to the baker. He stopped by the blacksmith long enough to thank him for the oven and pans. As Jonathan was being escorted to the courtyard where the King was waiting, Jonathan became visibly nervous.

"Don't worry sir," laughed the escort. "You are far more apt to receive an award than to be hung. Your fame is reaching throughout the land."

Jonathan relaxed and regained his composure. He bowed deeply as he approached the King.

"Good afternoon," said the King. "I hear from the Baron and others that you are my most successful subject."

"The honor is greater than I deserve your highness," said Jonathan.

"So, tell me Jonathan, to what do you owe your rapid success?" asked the King.

Jonathan told the complete story from the beginning with the witches, finding the book, solving the riddles over the last two weeks and ended the story with his meeting with the Duke earlier today.

The King sat quietly then asked Jonathan if he could see the book. Jonathan opened his pack and handed the book to the King. The King spent a long time reading the book and he paid particular attention to Jonathan's notes.

Finally, the King replied, "You have truly deciphered the magic riddles of the book. The knowledge within these pages can surely bring success to the reader provided they study and apply the principles within it. I believe I can help you answer the Riddle of the Brook."

Jonathan listen intently as the King continued, "You must do as you have been doing by sharing your knowledge and helping others. We are all one under God. What we do to and for others will affect us many times over. The more you give the more you will receive until you become one with everyone. Your message must reach the young and the old. It is never too soon or too late to learn the principles of life. Take the book lad and share your success. I am sure I will hear from you many times in the future."

Jonathan was awed by the wisdom of the King. He placed his book into the pack, handed a bottle of Vegetable Fair to the King, said good-bye, and departed the courtyard.

Chapter 24
Summary Four

The next few days were busy as everyone completed the final preparations for the fair. The rolls were so popular that Heather's mother spent several hours a day helping make bread along with selling Vegetable Fair with Mrs. Jenkens.

All the beverage stands were profitable, and several days' stock were already prepared. Jeffrey and Michael spent their spare time arranging the purchase of product beyond the fair. Jonathan and the Baron started making plans for the storage of Vegetable Fair and preparing the cottage for restaurant operation. Everyone helped find employees for the Duke and other items necessary for the Duke's grand opening.

The day of the opening, the lodge had a full house. It was the finest party ever. Everyone had an excellent time. Jonathan noted the change in the spirit around the castle. He could not hear his own footsteps if he tried. That evening they all sat around the courtyard to talk.

"Tell us Jonathan, what have you learned from the book the last few days?" asked Mrs. Becket.

Jonathan opened the book and read his notes so that all could hear; "I learned that though I may desire to help everyone,

I must concentrate my efforts on those that want my help. I learned that we are all susceptible to our environment and we affect the environment around us. What I feel affects you and what you feel impacts me. I must always guard against the negative and reinforce the positive. I learned that I must never make excuses about not having time and I must not waste time. I must always find something to keep me busy. I learned that attitude plays a big role in success. You must maintain a positive attitude at all times. The job must be done anyway so you might as well enjoy what you do. I learned it is okay to be successful but at the same time you must be true to yourself. Do not put on an appearance to impress others only to deceive everyone including yourself. And finally, I learned there is a spirit grander than myself that encompasses everyone. I must meld in harmony with my fellow human beings to help create a world more beautiful than the one that I used to only observe."

There was silence in the entire courtyard as everyone noted in solemn acknowledgment the truth of Jonathan's words.

Chapter 25
Desire

Suddenly a page fell out, it was tattered, worn and frayed.

It floated gently through the air and on the table laid.

Jonathan folded back the page, the words he read aloud,

Something magic in the words excited all the crowd.

"ALL ATTEMPTS TO PRY THE LOCK WILL LEAVE YOU BOUND THE SAME, PLACE THE KEY WITHIN YOUR HEART AND LOOSEN UP THE CHAIN."

"What do you really want Jonathan?" asked the Baron.

"Success," replied Jonathan.

"Don't you see Jonathan?" asked the Baron. "You have missed something in the book. What do you want from success."

"I want a big business," replied Jonathan with a confused look.

"Remember when Heather asked you what you wanted Jonathan?" asked Mrs. Becket. "You said success and Heather said to be more specific. She asked for curtains, bright curtains with lace. She truly wanted them from her heart, and she got them. Then your desire for the cottage soon came true."

"Yes Jonathan," said the Duke. "You must find what you really want just as I have done, or you will never have major success. This must be the most burning desire of your soul."

"And when you find that desire and obtain that desire you must add a new desire to continue to grow," said the Baron. "Without pursuing your strongest desire within your heart, you will never loosen the chains blocking your success."

"So, what is your strongest desire today, Jonathan," asked the stable master.

"Once you find and seek what you want, business will be easy," continued the Baron.

"Heather!" shouted Jonathan. "I want Heather to be my wife."

The crowd joined in with such a noise that the shouts could be heard for miles. Heather embraced Jonathan and tears came to her eyes. The tears came slowly at first and then with deep emotion from both of them. Soon the entire crowd was silent, many with their own tears of joy.

Chapter 26
Knowledge

Heather was the first to break the silence as she asked, "Does the book have anything else to say Jonathan?"

"This is the last chapter; I shall read it aloud." Jonathan continued reading,

"IF YOU FIND YOU HAVE NO HOPE, YOU CAN'T SEE THE GLORY. YOU'RE MISSING SOMETHING IN THE BOOK SO REREAD THE STORY."

"I know the answer," said the Duke. "Don't quit! You must never give up!"

Everyone clashed their mugs together in a toast to success as they yelled in harmony, "TRY TRY AGAIN!"

THE BEGINNING

ABOUT THE AUTHOR

Roger F. Johnsrud was born in Kalispell, Montana. After retiring as a lieutenant commander with twenty years in the military, he designed a robotics technology that will revolutionize the electronics industry. During his tour in the military and shortly thereafter, he engaged in many different and diverse businesses, including but not limited to salesman, manager, engineer, teacher, consultant, multilevel marketing, owner, and motivational speaker.

His underlying desire is that all children have a chance to start learning the "keys to success" before they take the historical road to initial failure. (If you are an old child needing these principles, it is never too late to enjoy and learn.)

He hopes this book will compel the reader to finish the story in one sitting yet continue to study its principles for a lifetime.

This book is dedicated to all children ages eight to eighty so that they may have the Key to Success without waiting any longer.

ACKNOWLEDGEMENT

First, I would like to acknowledge Jesus Christ who has stayed with me all these years and provided the guiding principles of this book. My faith in Him has allowed me to endure and overcome all the obstacles in my life.

Second, I want to acknowledge the late Og Mandino, a friend, and the author of many delightful and motivational books. His style set the form of this book.

Third, I want to acknowledge the late Bob Proctor, also a friend and colleague. He and his book "Born Rich" motivated me to quickly bring the first edition to press. He actually printed and distributed sixty copies of my manuscript before it went to press, forcing action.

Forth, I want to acknowledge the late Dottie Boreyko a wonderful woman whose favorite saying provided the title for this book.

Finally, I would like to acknowledge the pain of many failures in my life, without which I would have never known the true pleasure and meaning of success.

www.ingramcontent.com/pod-product-compliance
Lightning Source LLC
Chambersburg PA
CBHW040828010826
48978CB00012BB/647